THROUGH WALTER'S LENS

Through Walter's Lens

A novel
by

SUSAN L. POLLET

Adelaide Books
New York / Lisbon
2020

THROUGH WALTER'S LENS
A novel
By Susan L. Pollet

Published by Adelaide Books, New York / Lisbon
adelaidebooks.org
Editor-in-Chief
Stevan V. Nikolic

For any information, please address Adelaide Books
at info@adelaidebooks.org
or write to:
Adelaide Books
244 Fifth Ave. Suite D27
New York, NY, 10001

ISBN: 978-1-952570-49-0

Printed in the United States of America

Dedicated to Walter, his wife, and to Amos

Contents

"Heaven finds an ear when sinners find a tongue."

–Francis Quarles, Poet, Born: 1592; Died: 1644

Prologue

My father, Walter, a post World War II Jewish photographer in Cologne, Germany, died at age eighty-one of advanced lung disease. He was a survivor of the Nazi concentration camps, and had been tortured and brutalized on every level. He had many secrets. He had many demons. He had a zest for life.

Friends tell me that I was fortunate to have spent concentrated time with him by his bedside during the months before he died. As I look back on it, as with everything in life, it had its flip side. We had a warm and loving father and son relationship, although I was more conservative and questioned his lifestyle and ethics, and he looked at me as too conventional. I was eternally the father, in fact, and he was the son. He did whatever he wanted to, and I was the responsible one. In the early years, I held the family together.

When I moved 3,760 miles away to New York City from Cologne, Germany, in my late twenties, never to return except for visits, I was no longer responsible on a daily basis, which was an immense freedom for me. Nonetheless, during those visits, when he came to New York to visit me, and over the telephone, I still bore witness to his exuberances, good and bad, and was called upon to help the family achieve stability.

Walter did not want to die, and was quite angry about it. His body gave out, yet his brain was still functioning as it had for him his whole life. During his last months, I took the opportunity to ask him all of the questions I had been holding inside for many years. He wanted to bare his soul. What he revealed was painful for me, because of his confessions of multiple affairs while he was married to my mother, his discussions of his gambling addiction, which he accepted as one does the color of one's skin, and all of his indiscretions, major and minor. Many of the stories I had already witnessed from the sidelines, either directly or indirectly in stories I heard from my mother, brother and family friends. Many of his memories were of the times he visited New York City.

We had all experienced Walter's intermittent disappearances for days at a time over the years. As he was about to die, he filled in what he was actually doing during some of those absences. Knowing how he spent his time, whether factual or fictional, was engrossing in that he said that he met many famous photographers throughout his life, including Lee Miller, Arthur Fellig ("Weegee"), Berenice Abbott, Walker Evans, Robert Capa, August Sander, Bill Cunningham, Diane Arbus, Henri Cartier-Bresson, Ilse Bing, Garry Winogrand, Cornell Capa, Helen Levitt, Alfred Eisenstaedt, Robert Mapplethorpe, Vivian Maier, Richard Avedon, Helmut Newton, and his wife Alice Springs, as well as the German artist Joseph Beuys. A few of those artists he met with me.

He provided me with not only lessons about him, but a personal look at some of the greatest photographers of all time. Although I never engaged in photography for a living, I was a journalist who covered the arts and photography. I have a passion for photography as a hobby, and a respect for those who have mastered it. I will credit my father for forever igniting my delight in it.

I wonder if he told me everything, and if everything he told me was real or imagined or some mysterious combination of his own making. I ponder if I could possibly have absorbed any more stories. I am forever processing what he did tell me. Perhaps I always will. My father made an art form out of his life. He always wanted his life to be bigger, and more interesting and exciting than it actually was. My hope is that after writing down these accounts, I will have more room in my head, and, perhaps, some measure of peace.

My father was convinced he would end up in hell because, he told me, that is where all his friends were. Wherever my father is now, perhaps I can give him more serenity in my telling of some of his experiences. I hope that he knew, during my bedside visits, that I truly forgave him for when he failed himself or others. Perhaps he ultimately respected me for following my own path and for being a different person than he was. I would like to think so.

I will always reserve a portion of my brain for kind thoughts about my father, whether he is viewed as a survivor, a sinner, a winner, a loser, an artist, or just a man, trying to live his life, in search of something even he, a consummate storyteller, could not completely articulate. This much I know. If he could have survived, he would have chosen to, with no regrets for how he lived his life, and little repentance for how he would continue to live.

Chapter One

A Born Photographer: Drawing with Light

"The personality of the photographer, his approach, is really more important than his technical genius."

–Lee Miller, American Photographer

During the months that I spent at the bedside of my father, while he was dying, I wanted to learn more about him as a professional photographer so that I could preserve that legacy for him, especially since he had been taking pictures for over sixty years. When I was a boy in Cologne, Germany, I accompanied him often, when he took photographs, and sometimes helped him to develop them in our darkroom in our home.

I asked him where he stored all of his photographs. I was shocked, and quite upset to learn that he had destroyed almost all of his photographs and negatives, except for a few hundred family photographs which he took, and professional photographs, a few of which I placed in this book. The photographs he threw away would have shown his artistic development from his early years in Manhattan in 1936 and 1937, before he was in Dachau, Buchenwald and Sachsenhausen Concentration Camps; from his time in Israel from 1939 to 1953; and from his subsequent years in Cologne, Germany from 1953 until he stopped photographing professionally in 1995. In addition, it would have included photographs of his European travels and intermittent trips to Manhattan throughout his life. After his death, I learned from my mother that he had taken many photographs of men and women in the nude, and perhaps he was embarrassed for others to find those. It did not explain the destruction of so many others.

When I asked him why he did not preserve his photographs, he said that he did not think that they were art, and he did not see any value in retaining them. I found this incomprehensible. He was a talented photographer, and had documented life, especially in Post World War II Germany, as few had. This made me want to know more about why he became a photographer, and about his life as a photographer, so that I might have a greater understanding of what it meant to him, and why he did not value his gift. This is his story as he told it, and as I interpreted it.

We began our "soul journey" when I asked him when his interest in photography emerged. He gave me a roundabout answer to that question. He said that when he was a teenager, living in an upper middle class Jewish home in Cologne, Germany, he had been expelled from school, gymnasium, primarily for being a Jew.

He said that soon afterwards, he needed to leave Germany for his own safety after an altercation with members of the Nazi party who had been sent to beat him up by his German non-Jewish girlfriend's father. He had been confined by the secret police, the Gestapo, in the El De Haus in Cologne, an interrogation prison, where he was questioned and tortured. He was thrown down the stairs, and beaten with chair legs and leather straps with hooks. He was kicked, beaten again, and dunked in a large water barrel so that the Gestapo could get rid of the blood and assess the injuries. Then they beat him some more.

In the weeks he spent in that prison, he did not have a shower and barely ate. He was called names such as Communist and Jewish pig. He heard other prisoners, young people, being tortured on a daily basis, multiple times per day. Their screams stayed with him as did his own fears. He was not permitted to see his family. Eventually, he was released. He did not want to experience more of that, and so he planned his departure from Germany.

Lee Miller

In early 1937, at the age of eighteen, he found employment on a transatlantic cruise ship between Bremerhaven, Germany and New York. While on the ship, he met a woman photographer, Lee Miller. It was that chance meeting, and the relationship that developed between them on the cruise, that planted the seeds for a profession for him as a photographer, which lasted for his lifetime.

Even though Walter had been traumatized by his experiences, he still retained a youthful innocence and a joie de vivre that even the Gestapo could not kick out of him. In the way of young people everywhere, he wanted to enjoy life, and because of having been tortured, he went at it with an intensity. Walter was extremely good looking. He had dark, wavy black hair, an olive complexion, a thin but muscular, wiry build, soulful eyes, and strong features. He was the precursor to Marlon Brando as a young man in "A Streetcar Named Desire." He had the sensitivity of an artist, and had many female aspects to his personality. He was friendly, open, generous of spirit, comedic and highly intelligent. He wanted positive adventures and an escape from the repression and oppression in Germany, and from his wounds.

Walter was confident and worldly for his years, a "bad boy," and a bit of a gigolo in the making. Many of the women on the cruise were attracted to him, and he had sexual encounters with a number of them. Some of these women were lonely, some were bored, and some were looking for excitement with a young man who was more than willing to provide them with what they wanted. He was surprised at how easy it was for him to get women to want sex with him, and he took full advantage of it. In fact, they were throwing themselves at him, or so he said.

From the moment the passengers boarded the ship, Walter noticed a woman he later learned was an American named Lee Miller. She was about thirty years old at the time and strikingly beautiful. She fit within the Nazi concept of Aryan looks. She had pale skin, blond hair and blue eyes, ideal features, and a statuesque body. Her father, in fact, was of German descent, and her mother was of Scottish and Irish descent. People were gossiping about her on the ship for many reasons. She was married to an Egyptian man, but was traveling alone and was clearly behaving as a single woman might, flirting with everyone, male and female. She was clearly the most alluring woman on the ship.

Walter heard that she had been a model in Manhattan in the 1920's, and had appeared on the cover of Vogue magazine.

As one of the most venerated models of her time, she was photographed by many leading fashion photographers in New York, including Edward Steichen. Walter also heard that she, herself, was a famous photographer. She carried her camera, a Leica III, with her wherever she went on the boat. Walter was determined to meet her, as she fascinated him more than anyone else did.

His opportunity finally came on the third evening of the voyage when he spotted her alone on the ship's desk, taking photographs. Walter was extremely gregarious, and went right up to her and started to engage her in conversation. He learned that she recently came from Germany, where she had purchased her Leica camera. Walter asked her about her life, and how she had become a photographer, as he heard that she had been a fashion model.

That first evening, they sat on the deck talking until the sun came up. She had a bottle of alcohol she brought to the deck, which she shared with him. Walter had a warm personality and a loving heart. Even at that young age, he knew how to listen, and how to get people to feel comfortable to tell him their deepest thoughts. He sensed that even though Lee had the bravado of a stunning, accomplished woman, she had a lot of pain underneath.

After many drinks, Lee shared with him that when she was a young girl, age seven, she was raped by a family friend and infected with gonorrhea. She had to undergo treatments for the disease which included irrigation of the bladder and douching. On some level she never felt clean again, as if she were "damaged goods." And, unfortunately, there were flare ups of the disease in later years. Her deep sadness, and her description of drinking to excess during her adult life, made sense to him after hearing that. She had been exploited for her beauty many times in different ways, before and after that incident.

Lee told him that while she was growing up, her father, whom she claimed adored and favored her, used her as a model for his amateur photography and taught her the technical aspects of photography. She said, without emotion, that her father photographed her in the nude, even when she became a young woman. She shared how much she loved her father and did not criticize him for using her as a model. She seemed to justify it as part of the art.

Walter did not know what to make of that. He came from a traditional family. He was not sure what parental love was. His mother died when he was young, and he had been raised by his step-mother. She was a good caretaker, but he never felt that she loved him. His father was a conventional businessman, and could not relate to Walter's political attitudes and rebellion. Walter hated the Nazis, and rebelled against authority at every turn. Even in his ignorance of what a supportive family looked like, Walter felt emotionally that what Lee's father did to her was not right, especially since her father knew she had been raped at a young age. He did not want to judge it, but his instincts told him that she should not have been further sexualized in that way.

Walter understood why becoming a fashion model fit in with all that had happened to Lee. She was used to being the subject of the male gaze and objectified. He asked her why she stopped being a model. She shared that a menstrual pad company used a photograph of her by the famous photographer, Edward Steichen, to advertise their product, without her consent. After that, her career as a model ended.

Lee told Walter that she had her own dreams and ambitions, and was not merely a victim of her circumstances. Her parents had instilled in her that she was capable, and she was primed for challenges. She moved to Paris in her early twenties in order to become an apprentice to the great photographer and surrealist artist, Man Ray. In addition to becoming his student, she became his model, collaborator, muse and lover. She told Walter about the photographic technique of solarisation she used with Man Ray, and how she started her own photographic studio in Paris. After she and Ray had a dispute over the attribution of work they did together, she moved to New York City in 1932 to establish her own portrait and commercial photography studio. She became highly successful. She had famous clients, and was included in important photographic exhibitions. In 1933, she had a solo exhibition. Although people, primarily men, tried to use her, she became adept at getting what she wanted out of each situation too.

Walter asked Lee if she could teach him some photography while they were on the ship. She agreed to meet with him every day of the voyage at a designated time while he was off duty. She showed him how to hold her 35 millimeter camera, which was a small, manual, handheld Leica camera, and how to shoot with it. It was among the first of its kind, and was easy to use. She instructed him on how to insert and cut the film. There were no film cartridges available yet. She showed him how to set the speed and the aperture as he had to learn how to gauge the light. Photography is all about light. There were no meters available then either. She taught him that in order to take good pictures of people, he had to stand close to them. She instructed him on how to look through the viewfinder and how to set people up in the correct positions to obtain the proper angle.

During the voyage, Walter took many photographs of the women he had liaisons with, and the crew. Because of his engaging personality, they were willing subjects. He even took some photographs of Lee, and she of him. He learned not to be afraid of people, and he composed the photographs like a painter would compose a painting. Lee helped him with his artistic and technical vision. He had his own innate abilities, too, and thus was an excellent student.

On the ship, they made their own darkroom in Lee's bathroom. She taught Walter how to develop the film. She had developing equipment with her which consisted of different chemicals including vinegar, rubbing alcohol, water, developer and fixer. They used the sink to wash the film and the tanks. After they developed the photographs in the dark with the different chemical solutions, they hung the film over the bathtub to dry. At that time, they were using black and white film. Walter was able, eventually, to help Lee develop all of the films both she and he had been taking. She taught him how to look at the negatives with an enlarging glass.

Within a short time, Walter, a natural, became adept at composing and taking photographs, and developing them. He had talent, and Lee praised him for it. Her heart went out to him when he described the discrimination he, his family, and community had faced in Germany because they were Jews. He told her about how he had been vilified and tortured by the Nazis. He talked about his affinity for the downtrodden, the outcasts, the other, the homosexuals, the gypsies. She felt useful giving him a tool for seeing life in a new way which would help him to navigate the world and his future. Walter was able to relate to people easily, and that gift enabled him to bring something about their inner life to the surface when he took pictures of them. He could also see the beauty or interest in a landscape, and could heighten what other people might not see at first glance.

One day while they were talking, Walter asked Lee what had happened to her studio in New York, and if she was going back to it at the end of the voyage. She told him that she left her studio in 1934 to marry her husband. She thought that he would give her stability. She went to Egypt with him and did not work as a professional photographer there but did take photographs for herself. She told Walter that she did not like living in Cairo, and she missed her work, her independence and her freedom. She found marriage too constraining, and her role as a woman in Egypt confining and stifling. It was clear that for her, the marriage was over.

She shared that she had returned to Paris alone and met a British painter and curator, who became her lover. It turns out that he had had mostly male lovers prior to her. At that time, she became, also, a muse for Picasso and the darling of the surrealists and exhibitionists. That group was free with self expression, nudity, sex and drink. They defied convention and did what they pleased, regardless of the then prevailing societal norms. That attitude appealed to Walter. She said that she had been in Germany on holiday with her lover before she took this trip to New York. She was planning to see her family in New York, but was hoping to leave her husband on a more permanent basis, and return to Europe to be with her lover.

When Walter lived in Germany, he did not know any people like her. She was trying to be a modern woman in a way that he had not experienced in his young life. As Walter learned more about Lee, he realized that her greatest desire was to be artistically and sexually free, but as he listened to her discussions about her liaisons and relationships with famous and not-so-famous people, he did not see total freedom in it for her.

One night, after they both drank a lot, they finally had sex. He made certain that she wanted to do it, as he felt deeply for her as a friend, and was aware that she had been used by men in the past. He valued her as a teacher and companion more than anything. Although she was trying to be a free spirit, he felt that there was a holding back in her, as if she was not really there while they were having sex, but rather was floating above on some ethereal cloud. He knew when someone was truly present with him, even in an animalistic way, and when not. She told him that she felt like a fiend inside, despite her outward beauty. It was hard for Walter to fully understand that.

After that experience they had sex a number of times. While it was sweet, because of their mutual affection, he almost felt sorry for her. Because of his sensitivity, he could feel the continued trauma of her having been raped in her lovemaking. It was as if she was numb, or not present on some level. She had a separation of body from spirit. She was daring, but without the true caring on her part, it was not a real connection for her. She was confused about what she wanted, and from whom. Her body was not truly free. He felt that they had a deep emotional, but not a physical connection.

After the ship arrived in New York, Walter and Lee vowed that they would try to keep in touch. Walter gave her his family's address in Germany, and she gave her family's address in New York, as neither had a stable residential address at that moment. Walter ended up in several different Concentration Camps, including Dachau Concentration Camp, in 1938. Lee was living in London with her lover at the outbreak of World War II in 1939.

After Walter was released from Dachau in 1939 and moved to Israel, he wrote to Lee and told her what had happened to him. The letter was forwarded to her by Lee's father. She was experiencing the bombing in London at that time. Inspired by Walter's story and her own experiences, she was determined to become an official war photographer, which she did, for Vogue magazine. In 1945 she went to Cologne, Germany, which had special significance for her because she recalled conversations she and Walter had about his years growing up there. She interviewed many civilians and took photographs of the spires of the famous cathedral, with the city flattened by bombs around it. She told Walter, in correspondence, that of all the people she spoke with in Cologne, no one admitted to having been a Nazi or to having supported Hitler. She felt that they were unable to tell the truth and became fiercely anti-German after that.

One of her assignments was to photograph the Nazi Concentration camps at Buchenwald and Dachau. She begged for the assignment because she felt that it was important to show the world what had happened to Walter and others. She took photographs of piles of corpses; the trains, still full of bodies, surrounded by flies; the human bones; and the survivors. She remained forever traumatized by what she smelled, saw, and photographed. She wrote a letter to Walter acknowledging all he and his people had suffered. In a famous staged photograph from 1945, a copy of which Lee sent to Walter, Lee is pictured in Hitler's bathtub in Munich. She later slept in Hitler's bed. Walter understood the irony of the image, and the acts.

She was disturbed, on some level, to learn later on that he moved from Israel back to Cologne, Germany in 1953. Walter said that he and Lee corresponded, intermittently, until she died in 1977, but never saw each other again. After World War II, she remained in Europe, and covered the aftermath of the war in Eastern Europe. Walter was residing in Israel from 1939 to 1953. Lee finally divorced her Egyptian husband in 1947, and then immediately married her British lover, with whom she remained married until her death. Her only child, a son, was born in 1947. They resided in England. Even though Walter ended up living in Cologne, Germany from 1953 on, Walter and Lee never sought to arrange a visit. Their connection was emotional and spiritual, not physical. They sent each other photographs and news of each other.

Walter learned that Lee suffered from debilitating post traumatic stress disorder, as did he. While Walter continued to be a photographer until the end of his life, Lee gave it up to become a gourmet cook. She had trouble with alcohol at certain points, and continued to suffer from depression after what she had seen and witnessed during the war and perhaps from her early traumas. Walter had a gambling addiction, and often got his family into financial trouble because of it. She confided in Walter by letter that she was extremely upset because her husband was having a long-term affair. Walter tried to console her, and admitted his affairs to her. He told her that he still loved his wife despite them.

After my father told me the stories of his relationship with Lee Miller, I researched and learned that Lee's son had discovered approximately sixty thousand photographs, negatives and other documentation, including letters, in boxes and trunks in her attic after her death. This made me mourn the loss of my father's photographs all the more. He did not retain her letters either. Lee Miller did not promote her own work during her life, nor did my father. It was up to me to do it, and I cannot. But knowing that he initially learned how to take photographs from Lee Miller, and that she was inspired to become a war photographer because of what had happened to my father and others during the war and in the concentration camps, makes me grateful. My only regret is that they each suffered so from what they had seen, endured and photographed.

Chapter Two

Gotham, 1937-1938

"To me, pictures are like blintzes-ya gotta get 'em while they're hot."

–Weegee (Arthur Fellig), American Photographer

"Photography helps people to see."

–Berenice Abbott, American Photographer

"Whether he is an artist or not, the photographer is a joyous sensualist, for the simple reason that the eye traffics in feelings, not in thoughts."

–Walker Evans, American Photographer

After my father said goodbye to Lee Miller and left the ship, which had landed in Hoboken, New Jersey, he found his way to his paternal aunt's apartment. She lived on Eastern Parkway in Brooklyn, New York. Lee, in turn, travelled to her family's upper middle class home in upstate New York. Despite Walter and Lee's different upbringing and cultures, they had an affinity for one another, as artists and humanists, which lasted until her death.

Walter's aunt offered to let him stay with her indefinitely, on her couch, but he was employed on the ship, and did not have the proper visa. He went back and forth from New York to Germany about ten times between 1937 and 1938. During those visits, he mostly prowled around New York City at night, and slept at his aunt's apartment by day. He obtained a "college education" about gambling, drinking and sex. He found that he liked sex with women and men. His aunt, on the other hand, was a simple person who peddled underwear in poor neighborhoods to make a living, and struggled. She was unaware of where he went, or what he did at night. She would have been horrified.

Weegee

Walter said that during those visits to New York in 1937 and 1938, he met several famous photographers who influenced him. The first was Arthur Fellig, also known as Weegee. Walter, like Weegee, was attracted to bookies, gamblers, madams, call girls, pimps, con men, and outcasts. He met Weegee for the first time at a seedy bar in the Lower East Side area of New York City. It was about 10:00 at night. Weegee was having a beer before he set out at midnight to take his photographs of people in missions, flophouses, drunk tanks in the jails, strippers and crime scenes. By sheer chance, Walter sat next to him at the bar, and they started to talk. Weegee was about thirty-eight years old at the time.

Walter learned that Weegee was Jewish, and also a jokester. They both had "larger than life" personalities, and started to bond immediately. Weegee told him that in 1909, when he was ten years old, he emigrated with his family from Zloczow, Galicia, part of the Austro-Hungarian Empire, which is in the Ukraine today, to New York City's Lower East Side. Walter shared with him stories of his family in Cologne, Germany, and how his father and brothers had moved to Brazil to escape the Nazis a few months prior. Walter loved Germany, thought he could fight the Nazis, and that he could wait it out until they were no longer in power.

They learned that they were both nonconformists, that they scorned the conventional, and that they had contempt for stay-at-home people. Weegee slept on park benches after he stopped living with his family at age eighteen. Walter, now that same age, did that too, when he lost all his money gambling, and had no money to travel back to Brooklyn.

They had another major proclivity in common, a love of photography. Weegee had no formal training. He learned exposure, developing and printing on his own, and on the job. He photographed life as he saw it. Weegee told Walter that he had started out as a street photographer of children whom he sat on his pony, that he worked as an assistant to a commercial photographer, and later as a darkroom technician for a news organization where he also did photojournalism when needed. Approximately two years prior, he began working as a freelance photographer. He had his "office" in the Manhattan police headquarters, and lived in a rented room on the street behind. When a story came over the police teletype, he would race the police to the scene, and often arrived there first. He would then sell his photographs to the tabloids and photographic agencies.

Walter told Weegee that he was lost in that he knew he did not want to be employed on a ship forever, but did not know how he could make a living. He did not want to live in Brazil with his father and brothers, and they did not want him there either. The Nazis would not allow him to become educated or to have a profession as a Jew in Germany. Weegee counseled Walter that photography was the easiest profession to get into. He said that editors are always looking for something human, something different, and that the door is always open to beginners and the unknown. Weegee saw that Walter had an engaging personality. He told Walter that in order to make photographs, you have to mingle with everyone, and you cannot just be polite. He counseled that "you have to go around and stick your nose into other people's business." Weegee was used to making "harsh intrusions upon private suffering."

Weegee's father, like Walter's aunt, struggled to support his family as a street peddler, and later fulfilled his life ambition of becoming a Rabbi. Walter and his family were not religious, and that would certainly not be a calling for someone like Walter. Walter's father and brother were conventional businessmen, and that was not Walter's style either. Weegee left school at age fourteen to help to support his family, and never looked back. Walter left school at age sixteen for different reasons. Walter, in hearing Weegee's story, started to have hope that he could have his own photography business someday.

Walter did not like rules, authority, or answering to anyone, nor did Weegee. Weegee would not wear a tie or conventional clothes of the time. Walter was the same way. The freelance life fit them both well. Over time, Walter thought of Weegee as an older brother, as Walter's blood brothers were too different from him in every way and disapproved of his personality, interests and conduct. On the contrary, Weegee encouraged Walter's errant behaviors.

Walter asked Weegee if he could follow him around some nights to the crime scenes and other locations to learn from him. Weegee was generous of spirit, and took Walter with him on many occasions, every time Walter came to New York during that period. Weegee loaned Walter an old camera that he could use to practice taking photographs. Weegee drove a battered car which had a radio tuned to the police-call wave band. He used a 4 x 5 Speed Graphic camera preset at f/16 at 1/200 of a second, which was a much bigger and bulkier camera than the Leica. He used flashbulbs and a focus distance of ten feet. Weegee knew which images would sell, and taught Walter about making the most of a scene, or staging one. They both had a flair for the dramatic.

Walter saw him take pictures of gruesome dead bodies, dead racketeers, newborns alive in trash cans, fires, truck crashes, drownings, lineups at police headquarters, vice raids, riots, burglaries, lovers, children, and grief-stricken people. He went with him everywhere in Manhattan, from Harlem to the Bowery, as Weegee was always looking for slices of life. Weegee loved the circus, as did Walter, and they were fascinated with the unusual people and events that took place at them. The circus performers were more than happy to let Weegee take pictures of them.

He watched as Weegee juxtaposed images of wealthy people with images of the city's downtrodden. He observed how Weegee took pictures of people watching a gruesome scene to heighten the mood. It was the time of the Great Depression in the United States, and people would read the newspapers so they could forget their troubles and learn about other people's troubles. Weegee's images provided the diversion all were looking for, "the bloodier and sexier the better," and the newspapers depended upon him for coverage.

Walter asked to see Weegee's files of photographs. He did not keep files, but put his extra prints and negatives into a barrel. Walter looked through those. Weegee took Walter to his favorite camera store on West 46th Street, and taught him about equipment. He also introduced him to celebrities of the time, such as Gypsy Rose Lee, who was an amateur photographer and frequented the store too.

Weegee taught Walter about all manner of nightlife in Manhattan. They went to such places as the first racially integrated nightclub called Cafe Society, located next to Sheridan Square, and they enjoyed Arthur's Tavern on Bleecker Street, a jazz club, in the West Village. There was a seedier night life they experienced together too. Weegee visited prostitutes and gambling joints, often. Walter followed suit. Walter began to see the world, more and more, through Weegee's eyes, a world of underworld figures and human behavior of every sort.

One place they liked to frequent was on West 116th Street in Harlem, because there were black and white prostitutes. Sex cost $1.00 per prostitute. Another place was on Amsterdam Avenue in the Seventies. None of the prostitutes spoke English, they seemed to have been smuggled off the boats from Cuba, and walked around nude so the men could more easily pick out the prostitute they wanted. Weegee introduced Walter to a lot of nurses whom he met while taking photographs at the hospitals. Weegee said that nurses had a "great capacity for love." Weegee picked up women from the street while he was in his car, and took them for joy rides. Sometimes Walter went along for the ride.

Weegee went to a nudist colony in New Jersey on the weekends in the Summer, and took many photographs of nudes there. He became their "official" photographer. He invited Walter along when Walter was in New York, and during the Winter, Walter went with him to an indoor swimming pool at Broadway and Ninety-Sixth Street where the nudists also met. Walter watched Weegee's technique for photographing nudes, and practiced some shots himself.

There was one thing Walter observed about Weegee that he could not relate to. Weegee worked constantly, whenever a story broke. There was at least one murder every night, and he covered most of them. It was a violent era, and he was determined to photograph the "soul of the city" as he saw it. He smoked twenty cigars and drank twenty cups of coffee every day. This was hard living, and Walter was not certain that he wanted to duplicate everything about Weegee's life style. On the other hand, Walter was impressionable, and observing Weegee made the thought of having a wife and family seem less attractive to him compared to the excitement Weegee experienced on a daily basis. This inner conflict continued for Walter throughout his adult life.

Berenice Abbott

There was an aspect of Walter which Weegee did not share. Walter was attracted to men sexually. During his visits to New York during 1937 and 1938, he participated in the hidden gay life there. He befriended many homosexuals and lesbians. Ironically, in 1939, New York City closed most of the well-known gay bars in preparation for the World's Fair. By that time Walter was in Dachau Concentration Camp.

When Walter was on the ship with Lee Miller, she told him about a famous woman photographer named Berenice Abbott who resided in New York City. Lee encouraged Walter to seek her out. Berenice was a self-proclaimed lesbian, and nine years older than Lee. She had studied art in Paris and Berlin. In 1923, she had been a darkroom assistant to Man

Ray in Paris, as Lee had been, and he allowed Berenice to use his studio to take her own photographs. She thereafter opened her own studio in her home and became a portrait photographer of many famous people including Andre Gide, James Joyce, Peggy Guggenheim, and Jean Cocteau. In 1925, Man Ray introduced her to the photographic work of Eugene Atget, a documentary photographer of Paris, many of whose prints and negatives she purchased at his death. She spent a lifetime promoting Atget's work, in addition to pursuing her own serious photographic career.

In 1929, Berenice visited New York City, and fell in love with it. She closed her studio in Paris and moved to New York permanently. She became less interested in doing portraits of people, and more interested in doing portraits showing a changing city, documentary photography, as Atget had done in Paris. She documented the old and new in New York, and photographed examples of beauty and decay. She used a large format 8 x 10 camera, and believed in unmanipulated photographs both in the subject matter and developing processes. She was part of the straight photography movement.

During one of his visits to New York, Walter met Berenice in a Greenwich Village loft which was the apartment of one of his gay friends. Berenice was a neighbor, and was accompanied by her female lover, with whom she lived, the art critic Elizabeth McCausland. Berenice was thirty-nine years old at the time, and had short, cropped hair, and big, doleful, feline eyes. She wore tailored, mannish clothing. Walter was attracted to her gender fluidity.

Walter and Berenice immediately started to talk when they were introduced to one another as individuals interested in photography, and after Walter mentioned to her that he knew Lee Miller. Berenice talked about Germany with him, also, as she had studied in Berlin. She was articulate, direct, and clearly an independent woman. She expressed to him that she did not understand why people did not like independent women, but she did not care. She was a teacher of photography also, and Walter admired her and wanted to become her informal student. They became friends. She was about as different from Weegee as a person could get, but Walter had a capacity to befriend people from all cultures, races, religions, milieus, and sexual orientations. That was his great gift.

Berenice told Walter that she was working at the Federal Art Project as a project supervisor for her "Changing New York" project. She also did commercial work and taught at the New School for Social Research. She invited Walter to go to the Museum of the City of New York with her to see her work, which had appeared in an exhibition called "Changing New York." It later became a book of photographs to show the physical transformation of New York City.

She also invited him to her loft, where she showed him some of her photographs, including pictures of a Bowery restaurant, the Manhattan skyline, homeless housing on the street, an automat, Pennsylvania Station, the Manhattan Bridge, a department store, Financial District rooftops, the Flatiron Building, a hot dog stand, and much more. One night, he accompanied her to the window of a skyscraper, where she had shot her photograph "Nightview, New York," to show him how she did it. He mentally compared what he had experienced firsthand riding around with Weegee, with how Berenice saw the City, and received a lesson from her about how the streets and buildings had changed in a decade.

Walter was impressed with her discipline, diligence, and artistry. She was opinionated, but he enjoyed her opinions, and he was not threatened by her as others may have been. She was her own person. He liked the fact that she had experienced sex with men and women, as he had. She had a great mind and was interested in math and science. Walter had been an excellent student in those subjects, and shared that passion too. She was fascinated by the technical aspects of photography, and talked to Walter about that. Berenice did not come from a wealthy family and Walter's family had lost their money and possessions to the Nazis in Germany. If Walter wanted to become an artist, he would have to work too, and photography would allow him to become a working artist. He saw that Berenice had to take photographs of weddings and children to survive. He knew that she struggled financially in order to support her passions. Unlike Berenice, Walter did not think of himself as an artist.

He decided to attend a few of Berenice's photography classes at the New School. He learned more about light, shadows, how to photograph dynamic angles, as well as learning her darkroom skills including intentional cropping. He met an older, wealthy gay man, an art dealer with family money, who attended the class. He was married, and had two children. Walter and he had an affair, and he wanted to keep Walter in New York and set him up in an apartment. Walter considered it, but he always went back to Germany on the ship. He felt himself to be bisexual, and was not certain that he would have enough freedom as a "kept man." In any event, his immigration status made that choice impossible for him.

Walker Evans

The last famous photographer Walter met in New York City during that period was Walker Evans. Evans was about thirty four years old at the time. Berenice invited Walter to attend a small dinner party at her loft. Walker Evans was a guest also. They sat next to one another and shared a long conversation. Evans, like Berenice, was obsessed with the photographic work of Eugene Atget, and he often spent time with Berenice going through her collection of his work. He shared with Walter that he revered Atget's unsentimental style, and thought that art should conceal its art. He told Walter that another of his influences was August Sander, who was a German photographer. Ironically, August Sander became a great friend of Walter's in the 1950's, and developed most of Walter's photographs at his shop.

Evans told Walter that for the last year, he had received a regular salary from the Farm Security Administration to photograph rural America, primarily in the South. He wanted to show the character of American culture at that time. He had also done some work for Fortune magazine, which consisted of a study of a few sharecropping families in Alabama. Unlike Weegee, he did not want to intrude into the lives of these people, but rather, wanted to collaborate with them and to make them comfortable when photographing them. Walter realized that Evans was truly a pioneer of documentary photography.

Evans invited Walter to go to the Museum of Modern Art to see a retrospective exhibition of his work. The book which accompanied the exhibit consisted of eighty-seven photographs Evans took between 1929 and 1936. Much of the work was done with a large-format 8 x 10-inch view camera. Evans also photographed with Leica and Rolleiflex cameras. Walker told Walter that he had selected all of the images, a third of which were the photographs he took of rural America. He had not intended for the work to be a social protest. Rather, he was just shooting what he saw. Walter, who had an affinity for the powerless, the disadvantaged, and the underprivileged, was moved by Evan's portrayal of the Great Depression, and of rural poverty and misery.

Evans told Walter that his photography was as much about luck as it was about skill. He told him that he had received his visual education from his painter friends, and that Walter should study great paintings for their treatment of composition, light and color, but not to be overly concerned about the technical, and to work from instinct. He told Walter that he was against salon, beauty and art photography, which were the accepted aesthetic when he started out, and that he took his own path by photographing ordinary things, people, signs and lettering. He felt that he was doing something valuable, and he felt comfortable pioneering both aesthetically and artistically. Walter learned that being a rebel could be an advantage. He was also attracted to ordinary life, and that is exactly what the photography of Evans captured so well.

Around that same time, Evans had begun to experiment with street photography. He started to take photographs in the New York City subways with a camera hidden in his coat. On a few occasions, Walter went with him, to observe his technique, to scout out interesting subjects, and to divert people so that Evans could get effective shots. Evans gave Walter a Leica camera to use, which Walter felt comfortable with since Lee Miller taught him to use it, and he experimented on his own.

Sometimes Evans would engage with the people in the subway and on the street, and ask their permission to photograph them. He observed how Evans was able to relate well to people because he was interested in their lives, asked questions, listened, and sometimes explained why he found them photographically interesting. His subjects participated and cooperated, so that the result was less artificial. Evans told Walter that he should not be afraid to photograph the ugly, the shocking, and the brutal. He counseled that what Walter should Go for are images that are real and memorable, and which would stand the test of time.

Evans taught him that the only way for him to become truly proficient at photography is to keep experimenting and to spend a lot of time doing it. He suggested that he speak with other photographers and study their work, but to be guided, ultimately by his own unique vision. Evans was a great reader and writer, and he brought that to his visual work. Evans had others spend time in the darkroom making prints from his negatives, unlike Berenice. Walter realized that he would have to find his own style. He needed to spend his time focusing on the aspects of photography he found most compelling.

Immediately before Walter left on the ship back to Germany, for what turned out to be the last time, he engaged in activities he liked the best in New York City. He went to Times Square and observed all of the hustlers, pimps and prostitutes. He observed the three card monte games on the street for hours, and lost almost all of his money. He and Weegee went on a few more orgiastic sprees.

Walter was most interested in the people on the edge of society, and felt more comfortable with them. In the past few years he had become a combination of Lee Miller with her deep traumatic pain, from having been tortured in Germany; Weegee with his penchant for the underworld, gambling, and enjoyment of sex, pulls Walter had felt all his life; Berenice with her practical approach to surviving through photography, which Walter later followed; and Evans with his attraction to ordinary people and their lives, a personal and political philosophy Walter had adopted from an early age.

What happened next in Walter's life threatened to destroy his body and soul. It was photography that saved him.

Chapter Three

Dachau Concentration Camp in 1938 and Israel from 1939 to 1953

"We who lived in concentration camps can remember the men who walked through the huts comforting others, giving away their last piece of bread. They may have been few in number, but they offer sufficient proof that everything can be taken from a man but one thing: the last of the human freedoms – to choose one's attitude in any given set of circumstances, to choose one's own way."

–Viktor E. Frankl, an Austrian Neurologist and Psychiatrist as well as a Holocaust Survivor

"In Israel, in order to be a realist you must believe in miracles."

–David Ben-Gurion, Primary National Founder of the State of Israel and the First Prime Minister of Israel

*"I hope to stay unemployed as a war photographer till
the end of my life."*

–Robert Capa, War Photographer and Photojournalist

My father told me that when he arrived back in Germany in 1938, he was immediately arrested when he disembarked from the ship. The Nazis transported him to Dachau Concentration Camp as they had records indicating that he was a Jew. He was also politically to the left, and he was being punished for that as well. He did not want to talk about that part of his life. I believe that he wanted to spare himself and me.

He repeated what he had told me over the years. He said that although he had been tortured and starved there, what he preferred to remember was that he met the most famous intelligentsia from Germany and many brilliant, interesting prisoners with diverse political views whom he probably would never have encountered in life outside the camp. My father was not political in the sense that he belonged to any party, but his version of "left wing" was that the downtrodden had to be supported and that the rich people were to blame for many of the problems in society. He was part of a gay group there too, many of whom were artists, photographers, lawyers, and free thinkers. They were all imprisoned after Hitler assumed power and the Nazis had control.

He told me that he was a jokester, even in concentration camp, and did somersaults to entertain the SS men. He tried to be friendly with everyone, even the German guards. Jews received some of the worst labor assignments, and were tortured more brutally. They were subject to the harshest treatment in all ways, including their housing, food, clothing, lack of bedding and lack of medical care. He was forced to wear two triangles creating a Jewish star on the left side of his striped jacket. One was the yellow triangle of a Jew, and the other was a pink triangle of a homosexual. He should have worn a third because he was considered a political dissident, but somehow they forgot that one. Miraculously, despite the labels he had to wear, Walter was spared some of the worst tortures because of his personality, and due to sheer luck.

Walter observed that one SS man had a Leica camera and took official photographs in the camp of visiting dignitaries, including Heinrich Himmler, Commander of the Special Police; General Von Epp; Bavarian Minister of the Interior Wagner, and others. Walter told him that he knew a lot about Leica cameras, and that he was a photographer. They had many conversations about their mutual interest, and they learned about photography from one another. The SS man had a heart, and the soul of an artist, and was not in favor of the brutality he witnessed. He would sneak Walter some extra food from time to time.

The SS man also took photographs of some of the worst crimes against humanity. He told Walter he wanted people to see what really happened there. Walter did not know if all of those photographs ever made it out of the camp. The only photographs of Dachau that Walter saw later were the official photographs, including those of the visiting dignitaries, and one of an elderly man who was subjected to the standing torture, when the guards required a prisoner to stand for inordinately long periods of time.

Walter saw, later, the heart wrenching photographs of the prisoners and environs at Dachau when the prisoners were liberated by the United States Army, including those taken by Lee Miller. Walter did not know if the SS man remained in Dachau until it was liberated, or was stationed somewhere else, or died in combat. He tried to locate him after the war, but was never able to find him.

Walter left Dachau in 1939. I asked him how he managed to get out of the concentration camp. He claimed that he was found in bed with another young man in Dachau, and that he was then tried as a homosexual in Munich in what he called a "show trial." The Nazis wanted to show that Jews and homosexuals were evil people, and Walter had both strikes against him. After he was convicted of homosexuality, he was sent to prison for several months in Munich. Upon his release from prison, he was told to leave Germany within forty-eight hours. They released him to the general public as they did not realize he came from Dachau.

Because of the Nazi takeover, Walter's second eldest brother had emigrated to Palestine in the mid 1930's. Walter did not want to emigrate to Brazil where his other brothers and father had relocated, so he decided upon Palestine as his destination. He was certain that he would not be able to go back to New York because immigration was severely restricted. I asked him how he was able to afford to take the ship from Germany, and he told me that he hid some money before he went to Dachau, and he went and picked it up.

Palestine/Israel: 1939-1953

When Walter arrived in Palestine, he was penniless and homeless. His brother, who was already living there, was impoverished and shared one room with many other people in Tel Aviv. There was no space for Walter. He slept on roofs, on the beach, on benches, on the street, or wherever he could find shelter. He washed himself in the public bathrooms, and stole food and whatever else he felt he needed to survive. He tried to find jobs, but it was not easy at that time. He sold ice cream and corn on the beach, and did gardening. When he did have a little money in his pocket, he went to illegal gambling joints in Haifa, Tel Aviv and Jerusalem. Women always liked him, and he found many to have sex with. They were all lonely refugees, seeking comfort in one another. He lived that life until 1942.

Walter was a gentle soul, but he had to do what was necessary to survive and to support his fellow Jews. In 1942, Walter joined the British Army and became part of the Jewish Battalion to fight the Germans. He was stationed in Northern Africa, and he served until the end of the war in 1945. While there, he interrogated German prisoners of war. He was also a messenger, and drove around on a Harley Davidson motorcycle.

He returned to Palestine and joined the Haganah, a Jewish paramilitary organization, ironically, to fight the British who then occupied the area, which he did from 1945-1947. He said that his greatest trauma of that time was seeing one of his best friends blown up in a car directly in front of him. He knew that he could not fall apart, and had to stay strong and keep going like so many others around him.

In 1947, he decided that he needed to get away and wanted to obtain a job on an Israeli cargo ship called Zim. He was able to find employment as a sailor, and did menial tasks such as cleaning the deck. The ship arrived in New York. He left the ship and went to houses of prostitution and to gambling joints. As Walter told it, he lost track of time, the ship left without him, and he was homeless in New York for one month. He met several times with Weegee and Berenice Abbott, who both encouraged him to start doing photography again, which gave him inspiration. He spent most of his time in Times Square for escape. Finally, he met a man who was working on a ship on the docks. He helped Walter to get a job on a ship which sailed to France to pick up refugees, and then went to Cyprus. Eventually Walter wanted to return to Palestine. He was able to get on a ship to take him there. When he arrived in Palestine, he snuck in.

In 1948, he joined what became the official Israel Army, to fight the Arabs, shortly before Israel was declared a State in May of 1948.

He would not give me more details about what he saw in those three wars, but he said he saw enough hatred, violence, bloodshed and torture, coupled with what he had already experienced in Germany, to give him nightmares for the rest of his life. It was too many years of violence for a young, artistic man to absorb. There were many other Jews in Israel from throughout the world who had experienced as much as he did, and some endured more. That did not console him.

Robert Capa

In 1948, Walter met the war photographer, Robert Capa, in Tel Aviv. Capa was there to photograph the ceremony of the Declaration of the State and the Proclamation of Independence, to cover the War of Independence, and to photograph the leaders, the ordinary people, and the scenes of the street and countryside at a crucial time during the birth of Israel. Capa re-visited Israel several times in 1949 and 1950, and spent time with Walter when he did so.

They initially met at a cafe in Tel Aviv where many artists congregated. They were both dark haired and good looking. Walter learned that Capa was five years older than him, and that he was born Endre Friedmann in Budapest, Hungary. They both came from assimilated Jewish families. Capa, when he was a teenager, was accused of being a communist sympathizer, and fled Hungary and the political repression there. He told Walter that he had been arrested by the Hungarian secret police, beaten and jailed. With the aid of a family friend, he was released, and told to leave the country immediately. They shared a similar history of having been idealistic, non-religious Jewish youths who were persecuted for their religion and politics.

Capa told Walter that he moved to Berlin, Germany. He enrolled in college to study political science, and he had the ambition to be a writer. He was penniless and stateless, so he earned his living as an apprentice in a photography lab while attending college. When Hitler came to power, he moved to Paris because in Germany Jews were banned from colleges, and were restricted in so many other ways. Both he and Walter were continuously on the run at a relatively young age.

They discussed their empathy for other people, and how much they disliked war. Capa shared his experiences covering the Spanish Civil War, the Second Sino-Japanese War, and World War II across Europe. Capa believed in being close to the action. He took photographs, for example, from the trenches, and placed himself in harm's way many times. Capa's photographs had been published in major magazines and newspapers, and he had become famous, in part, because of the immediacy of his images.

Walter told Capa all that he had been through in Germany, New York, and Dachau. He spoke with Capa about the challenges of living in Palestine, and his trauma from having fought in three wars. On a lighter note, Capa had been in New York City at the beginning of World War II before he went off on assignment, and they exchanged stories about the life there.

They discussed how they had both escaped from Nazi persecution, and had struggled to survive. Capa told Walter how he could use photography both as a means of expression, and to change attitudes toward acts of violence. In that sense he was like the SS man in Dachau who witnessed and took photographs of what happened there. Walter and Capa both sympathized with leftists and were anti-fascist. Because Walter had experienced torture numerous times, and had served for so many years as a soldier, unlike Capa, he was not interested in covering war as a photographer.

Walter was not intimidated by Capa's accomplishments because Capa was unpretentious and spontaneous. They were brothers of an era. Capa wanted to photograph the "human condition," including the effects of war, even though he hated war. Walter did not believe that his own photographs were art, nor that they were worthy of being available to the masses. He was not motivated to become famous for his photography or for anything else. He was not interested in placing himself in danger in order to take photographs. He longed for a life of pleasure and calm. Capa had other ambitions, and was willing to take risks to his own physical safety to achieve them.

Capa told him about Magnum Photos, the organization he had co-founded in Paris with the French photographer, Henri Cartier-Bresson, and which was a cooperative agency for worldwide freelance photographers. Walter was not a joiner and was not interested. He merely wanted to work as a photographer to feed himself, and then to have lots of time off to gamble, to have affairs, to eat good food, to travel, and to spend his time as he pleased, without anyone telling him what to do. Walter, after having lost his youth to violence and hatred, did not want to spend any more time on organized activities of any kind, political, artistic, or otherwise. He did not want to follow orders. He was not interested in changing a world he did not believe could be changed because of human behavior.

Over the course of their many conversations, Capa shared with Walter many of his photographs of the people and scenes in Israel, which later were published in books. Walter was impressed with the human emotion expressed in many of the photographs in such an artistic way. Capa documented, too, the face of the land and the cities. Walter admired that Capa had captured that time in history well so that all who were not there could get a true piece of it.

Walter was particularly moved by Capa's photographs of soldiers walking on the road to Jerusalem to their fate during the war in 1948; war scenes on Tel Aviv beach; David Ben-Gurion reading from the Proclamation of Independence at the ceremony of the Declaration of the State of Israel; an improvised Menorah in the Negev desert; the people and streets of Jerusalem and other cities; immigrants at the Haifa port; people and scenes at absorption and immigrant transit camps; people engaged in ordinary activities such as working on a kibbutz in the field, giving and receiving a haircut, playing musical instruments, dancing, and painting on a canvas; scenes of the elections; and, most compellingly, close ups of the faces of the people from all over the world who had arrived in Israel with many different backgrounds and skills, and who were needed to quickly recover from the war to till the land, work the machines of the factories, and to speak one language, Hebrew.

Walter took note of the way Capa composed his photographs, his use of light, shadow, and angles, and his intimate portraits of people. What Walter learned from his discussions about photography with Capa was that if he approached the subjects of his photographs with warmth, and took the photographs close up, he could create an immediacy and intimacy which would make for a superior photograph. That was a lesson he adopted, and would keep perfecting, over the course of his life.

Married Life in Israel

Walter met my mother, who was also in the Army, they fell in love, and they married in 1949. She was a survivor of Auschwitz and Bergen-Belsen Concentration Camps and thus, they were able to understand and support one another. Nonetheless, Walter was conflicted. While he loved my mother, and was grateful that she cooked meals for him, washed his clothes, and took care of the little room they shared, he wanted to be able to do whatever he felt like without responsibility. Shortly after they married, he disappeared for a day or two. When he returned home he had a black eye. My mother learned that his best friend hit him because my father had abandoned his newly married bride to go gambling.

This was how my father behaved for his entire life. Walter felt that after all he had suffered, he was entitled to take pleasure no matter what the consequences. My mother mostly went along with it, although some of his indiscretions were hurtful. She provided him with a home base, with stability, with love, and with comfort. She took care of him. He wanted the freedom to prowl around at night, have his thrills, and return without having to explain himself.

After they had served in the Israeli Army, he moved to Haifa with my mother. She became pregnant within three months of their marriage, and I was born in 1950. Walter was raised to believe that it was his duty to support his wife, and soon to be born child, so he determined to become established in a business.

He started to do photography again out of his friend's apartment using a dark room set up there. His friend gave him a Leica camera to use. He took family portraits, and pictures of people at weddings and other religious ceremonies. He photographed people on the street who wanted it, and took photographs of commercial establishments and storekeepers. He went wherever he could find work, and began to be well known throughout Israel. He knew how to take candid shots, and how to make people pose and get them to have the expressions he thought would be most effective by using his charm. He knew how to set up a scene in a painterly way. His famous saying was to tell everyone, "moment, moment," while he composed the shot. He was close to a circle of bohemians, including writers, actors and artists. None of them had much money, but they knew how to relax together and celebrate life.

Walter was not someone who wanted to or was capable of leading a traditional married life. He was easy going and did not want to work too much. He told me that in 1952, when I was two years old, he met a beautiful redheaded woman who was sitting at a neighborhood cafe having coffee at the same time he was. He approached her, sat with her, and after a long conversation, followed her home to her apartment. He learned that she had been in a concentration camp, and that she was the mistress of an SS man who had saved her life and arranged for her escape. They were attracted to one another and had bonded from that first chance encounter. They had sex, and he did not think about his wife, my mother, at least not while he was with her. Walter felt constrained by the responsibilities of family life, and was looking for some relief.

When he returned home, my mother asked him where he had been. He had been missing for about five hours. He told her that he met a woman who had been in a concentration camp and that they shared stories. After much questioning by my mother, he finally admitted to having sex with her. He told her that it meant nothing to him, and was just a release. It is unclear if he was lying to her or himself. He carried on the affair two to three times per week for almost a year in what he thought was secret. It was an escape from family life and accountability. My mother heard from others that Walter was seen with this woman, and she herself caught them arm in arm walking on the street on one occasion. My mother insisted to Walter that they needed to move away, as she did not think her relationship with him would last with the other woman in the picture. He admitted to me that he loved my mother and had grown to love this other woman too. Walter never played by conventional rules. I wondered about the concept that you could love two people at once. There seemed to be pain for all in it. My father was amenable to leaving as he did not want to stay in Israel, but he insisted that they return to Germany.

In 1953, I left Israel with my parents to return to Cologne, Germany. I asked my father why he wanted to leave Israel, which was supposed to be a home for the Jews, to return to Germany where they did not want Jews to exist. Walter told me that he did not believe that there would ever be peace in Israel. He told me that even David Ben-Gurion, the first Prime Minister of Israel, was quoted as saying:

"Everybody sees a difficulty in the question of relations between Arabs and Jews. But not everybody sees that there is no solution to this question. No solution! There is a gulf, and nothing can bridge it...

We, as a nation, want this country to be ours; the
Arabs, as a nation, want this country to be theirs."

My father thought of Germany as home despite all that
had happened to him and others. His family had lived there for
centuries. He did not feel comfortable in the climate in Israel,
he was sick with malaria and felt he could not be properly
treated in that heat, and, most importantly, he did not want
to spend the rest of his life in a war-torn state. As a gambler,
he was willing to take his chances in Germany. My mother
wanted to leave Israel for her own reasons. She agreed to move
to Germany for my father, but was frightened to go there and
did not really want to. She loved him and wanted to keep the
family together, so she emigrated once again.

Chapter Four

Cologne, Germany

"Pure photography allows us to create portraits which render their subjects with absolute truth, truth both physical and psychological. That is the principal which provided my starting point, once I had said to myself that if we can create portraits of subjects that are true, we thereby in effect create a mirror of the times in which those subjects live."

–August Sander, a German Portrait and
Documentary Photographer

Upon returning to Cologne, initially, my father was too sick with malaria to work, so my mother had to support us by working at a factory. My father took care of me as best he could. Although I cannot remember that time as I was too young, my overall feeling about Walter has always been that he was patient, available, easy to talk with, sociable, and fun loving. He was more like a free-spirited older brother than a father, much of the time.

I asked him why he did not return to school after the war. He said that by the time he returned to Germany, he was too old to continue his studies, and he had a family to support. It was not an option. In any event, after everything he had endured, he could not picture himself in a classroom.

Once Walter felt better, he decided to become a full-time photographer in Cologne. He brought his Leica III camera with him from Israel. I asked him why he chose to continue to do photography. He said it made his life more interesting, it allowed him to have a profession, it was easy to do, he could bring his camera wherever he went, and it did not take up much space. For him, it was the perfect profession because the camera was always with him. He reasoned that there were not too many jobs where you could carry your equipment with you easily. He appreciated that he did not have to go to school for it, he could develop skills over time, and he could learn from other people, as he had been doing. It was not an artistic endeavor for him, but more of a survival mechanism.

He used a Leica III initially. There was a photography exhibit each year in Cologne starting in the 1950's called Photokina, where cameras were exhibited. Walter went to it for the first time in the Spring of 1954. From that time on it was biennial. In 1956, at that exhibit, he bought the Leica M3 at a reduced price. In 1969, he obtained a special edition of the Leica M4 at Photokina, which he used for the rest of his life. It had a black enamel finish and it commanded a premium from collectors because there were not too many made at that time. He did not believe in having complicated equipment. I still have it, and it is one of my prized possessions.

I asked him how he started his business in Germany. He said that initially he took photographs of people on the street, and then would ask them for money. He showed customers examples of other photographs he had taken. Everybody liked his work. They were drawn to his friendly, upbeat personality, and it was relatively effortless for him to make a sale. Over time, he expanded into many other venues. He always walked around Cologne with his camera dangling from his hand in search of opportunities.

Cologne was and is a city of pubs. There was at least one pub on each street corner, then and now. The famous beer sold in Cologne was Kölsch. For decades, you could not buy it in bottles, but had to go to the pub to drink it. The beer was distributed from large wooden kegs or directly attached to a brewery, of which there were dozens in Cologne, and was piped in directly. Walter did not drink much alcohol, but he preferred to go to places where people congregated, and the pub was one ideal locale. The pubs had different social groups depending on the neighborhood. Walter went to them all, especially when there were celebrations. Throughout the year, many celebrations provided Walter with the opportunity to enter and take photographs. He took the money for the photographs in advance, he would get the customers' addresses, and then mail them the photographs.

One of his major sources of income were the local Catholic hospitals, of which there were several. He would find out when the christenings would take place. There were usually several throughout the week, as they organized them in groups rather than individually. He would take photographs of christenings, and sell them to the parents and to other family members.

Walter was also a regular photographer for synagogue functions for Bar Mitzvahs and weddings. There were very few events, as there were not many Jews left in Germany after the war and the Nazi extermination. The parents would ask him to come to take photographs, and then he was paid by the parents who organized the function.

Another important venue for his business were the trade fairs. Cologne was a major hub for trade fairs, and there were many of every variety, from photography, to home goods, to furniture, to fashion, to food. Hardly a week went by without there being one. The annual food trade fair was called Anuga, which was a five-day event, and was the world's leading trade fair for food. I have many memories of accompanying Walter to the fairs. Throughout his entire career, Walter never obtained a license to take photographs, even though he was supposed to have one. He refused to have anything to do with German bureaucracy. For most venues, it was not checked, but I can recall that he was told to leave a few trade fairs because he did not have one.

While at the trade fairs, Walter would wait for an announcement that a top-ranked politician was present. It was a tradition that top-ranked politicians would attend the fairs, walk around, and visit several of the booths. He took photographs of the Mayors of the City of Cologne, including Theo Burauen, who was Mayor from 1956 to 1973. Walter became good friends with him. The politician who was liked the most for being "down to earth," was Konrad Adenauer, the former Chancellor of the Federal Republic of Germany from 1949 to 1963. Prior to the Nazis, he was the Mayor of the City of Cologne and had an extremely heavy Cologne dialect to which people could relate. Because Adenauer originally had his home in Cologne, and the Capital of Germany was in Bonn, about twenty miles south of Cologne, it was easy for him to attend the trade fair for food each year, and he made a point to be there. He knew Walter from the trade fairs.

Walter was known by everyone throughout the fairs as the photographer of visiting politicians. Walter photographed the politicians with the owners or employees of the company booths at the fair. He brought the photographs to the booths two days later. Not all owners of the booths were interested in the photographs, but most were.

He took photographs at the famous Cologne carnival each year, a traditional carnival which began in the eighteenth century. The weekend before Ash Wednesday was the big carnival weekend where there were many meetings of different carnival groups called sitzung. People would congregate in large halls, drink, listen to speeches and jokes, and watch dancing. The performers would wear medieval and other costumes, and sometimes the attendees would too. Often he would take pictures of groups, get the addresses of individuals in the groups, take their money ahead of time, and then send them the photographs. The more people he put in the picture, the more money he would get. He always developed a little less than the number of people in the photographs.

There were regular horse races in Cologne, and Walter frequented them. He was friendly with a large contingent of gypsies who went there often, and they became his friends. They would ask him to take photographs at gypsy funerals. At those funerals, they dressed the dead person in a complete outfit, including boots, in an open casket, and he was asked to take that photograph, as well as ones of the attendees of the funeral.

Like Weegee, Walter was attracted to all manner of people who were out of the mainstream of society. He took photographs of prostitutes and pimps on the street who would pay him for his photographs. In the 1950's and 1960's, there were several small streets in Cologne known to contain brothels. One of them was called Nächelgasse, the other one was called Kleine Brinkgasse. There were large walls which closed off those streets from view. Walter worked on the streets during the day and night several times per week. When our family had first arrived in Cologne, we paid a share for a large room in a building next to the Rhine River, which was next to one of those streets, so he had a long-term familiarity with the area. The prostitutes sometimes had sex with him for free, or he bartered photographs for sex.

What most appealed to Walter's sensibilities was that there was no typical day of work, and he only worked when he felt he needed the money. Each day held a new promise. Since there were regular fairs, he would go to them for a couple of days every few weeks. If he needed more money, he would go to the pubs, or the other venues. Sometimes he had appointments at events, but mostly he allocated his own time. On occasion he was paid for his work with watches and gold chains. He would bring unexpected items into our apartment which he had received in payment for his work.

Walter only worked a few days out of the month. My family was used to seeing Walter stay in bed, oftentimes throughout the day, most days. My mother brought him food in bed, and he remained there reading the newspaper and smoking cigarettes. Then he would switch to the bathtub and do more of the same. I never thought about why he did it. Upon reflection, I believe that because of his post traumatic stress syndrome, he needed a lot of down time when he did not have to interact with people or be responsible. And then, too, he wanted his own pleasures, and doing those things was a luxury for him.

The other reason may have been simple exhaustion from going out a lot at night to gamble at back alley gambling joints, and to have sex at the brothels and elsewhere. He gambled all of his life. There were many times when he would disappear for days when he went on a gambling spree. He liked to go to the casino and play roulette.

He was never upset about losing money, and would tell stories about it. He gambled away all of the family money, such that my mother insisted upon taking his earnings from photography, and hiding it away. Sometimes she forgot where she hid it. She did not want him to carry cash. My father made certain to keep some money for his gambling before he gave it to her. Many times we were dispossessed because Walter spent all the money, and there was none for rent. Often he had no money for gasoline. Walter did not care much about money other than it bought him a good time. He never felt badly about it. He needed excitement, he needed to live on the edge all of the time, and it never occurred to him to feel guilt.

He frequently spent time with actresses and artists in Cologne. He was part of the artistic community. My mother did not share that part of his life with him, nor did my brother and I. He was on his own, and my mother took care of us, primarily. Although my mother did not work, as there were no women working in the neighborhood, Walter did not feel the pressure. If there was no money, there was no money. His freedom meant more to him. They received a small amount of money from the German government, which was something.

When he was with the family, he was truly with us. Because he did not work regular hours, he spent a lot of time with us when he was not off doing his own thing. He encouraged us to get a good education as his was cut off so abruptly by the Nazis. To that extent he was parental. His favorite activity was to take photographs of family and neighborhood gatherings. He would not charge for those photographs, and sometimes gave poor people on the street free photographs. He took many pictures of our family on vacation.

My father had affairs all of his life. When I was school age, on one occasion my father was coming home from working a trade show, and he saw his neighbor putting out the laundry on the wire outside. She was living by herself on the next block, and was good looking. He was friendly and flirtatious, and asked her about her day. She invited him in for a cup of coffee. She became his girlfriend for about five years. My mother became friendly with her not knowing what was going on. My father said he broke up with the neighbor because of that, and that my mother never confronted him about it. I was shocked to learn this as part of my father's deathbed confessions.

Walter had another girlfriend, in 1955, who was married with two children. She was my mother's best friend. My mother and her friend went to a spa together and my father asked to join. Everybody was nude in the sauna as was the custom in Germany. Walter was attracted to her friend, and started a romance with her. My mother did not know. It went on for many years. Walter loved my mother but he also loved his life the way he wanted to live it. My mother eventually found out about the affair and Walter stopped the romance. He did not express any misgivings about having the affair, or, for that matter, about stopping it. He never played by the rules, and if rules were made for him, he would break them.

My father had many positive aspects despite what many would consider his sinful ways. Those qualities made him a good photographer. He had an easygoing relationship with my mother and was a caring father. He was patient, sweet, and gentle. He did not speak ill of others. He was sociable, he was fond of people, and people gravitated around him because he made them feel comfortable.

He was generous with his time, and made himself available when people needed him to drive them around, or do them favors. He was a loyal friend, and interested in people from different cultures and classes. He would talk a lot with friends into the night. They smoked cigarettes together and wrote each other letters. Sometimes he would go to pubs with them.

He had five to ten close friends throughout his adult life. Most of them did not have full- time jobs. He had gypsy friends that he formed friendships with in the late 1950's to 1960's. He had a close friend who was Persian. He was a friend from his days in Palestine, who ended up in London, England as a Professor in Literature. He kept in touch with a friend from a concentration camp who had moved to New York and was a consultant for a medical company.

Sometimes his friendships were made for practical reasons. At one point he befriended a German man who was the head of the Office for Reparations. He was friendly with his German psychiatrist who treated him for six to seven years. Walter wanted to be declared more incompetent so that he could get a larger disability check. Although he claimed not to need therapy, clearly, in retrospect, he did, since he had lived a lifetime before reaching thirty years of age. Much to Walter's dismay, his psychiatrist committed suicide before he had completed his therapy. My father did not want to talk about the suicide with me, or what it meant to him.

Walter's basic philosophy was to take life easy, to be merry, and to take things as they come. He was a Cologne person through and through, a Kölscher, a jokester who nonetheless took life seriously. He did not believe in God or organized religion. He never joined any groups, not even photography groups. His sympathies were with left wing groups, but he was not active politically. He defended Stalin even when information came out about Stalin's murders and purges in the Soviet

Union. He was progressive, and always voted for Communists. In his voting district, there were only three other communist votes on a regular basis. He was comfortable with being a minority and in the minority.

One of the most significant relationships for Walter in his professional and personal life was the one he had with August Sander, another Kölscher, who did the exposures of Walter's films for many years. Walter described him as an extremely nice man and as a gentleman through and through. They had a relationship which lasted until Sander died.

August Sander

From 1953 until August Sander died at age eighty-seven in 1964, Walter took his films to August Sander's photography shop in Cologne. Walter worked with him in the darkroom, and learned his technique for printing the pictures. Walter described the process which I was familiar with from when I accompanied him to the shop as a young boy. First the film would be developed, then it would be dried, and then a contact exposure of the film was made such that all thirty-six pictures were printed in the same size as the original film. Walter went to the lab, used a magnifying glass, and then chose the photographs that he thought were the best. He would order them by the number of the film, as each picture had its own identification number. Walter did some of his own developing, also, at home in his darkroom, as he knew the techniques first from Lee Miller, and then from August Sander.

Walter had many opportunities to speak with and to learn from Sander, who had long been a famous portrait and documentary photographer. Sander was the son of a mining carpenter, and had an affinity for documenting ordinary people going about their daily activities. By the time my father met him, Sander was no longer taking photographs. There was a forty-two-year age difference between them, and Sander treated Walter like a son. I remember that he had white hair, was overweight, and had a kind face.

Sander had been operating his studio in Cologne since 1909. He encouraged Walter to take many photographs, and to care about his subjects. He wanted Walter to be more than a commercial photographer, and to consider exhibiting his work, but Walter was looking at photography as a means to support himself and his family, and had no loftier goal, although he had the ability.

Sander was best known for his portraits, although his work included landscapes, nature, architecture and street photography. Unlike Walter, Sander, in his day, mostly took studio pictures with an old fashioned large format camera. He would expose the pictures on individual glass plates and used a long exposure time. Walter worked only with his handheld, small Leica camera.

In the 1920's, Sander was involved with an artistic movement, a group of progressive artists, including photographers and painters in Cologne, who sought to return to realism and social commentary in art. It was called Neue Sachlichkeit, or New Objectivity. Sander loved to recount memories of those times to Walter, and Walter was a good listener.

Sander had done a series of portraits for his books "People of the 20th Century" and "Face of Our Time," in the 1920's. His portraits were usually taken in natural light, and taken of the subject straight on. They were stark in appearance. He photographed German people from all walks of life and all social classes. You could tell what their class and profession was by their clothing and by the backdrop in the photograph. He grouped his portraits into seven categories which he labelled the farmer; the skilled tradesman; woman; classes and professions; the artists; the city; and the "last" people, which included such individuals as the elderly, the deformed and the dead, the homeless and veterans.

Sander's photographs included a wide range of humanity such as gypsies, farm laborers, circus performers, and prosperous businessmen and aristocrats. He created a record of life in Germany between 1911 and 1933 and a typological catalogue of more than six hundred photographs. By the early 1930's he gave radio lectures as he was recognized as an authority on photography.

Later, Sander suffered greatly under the Nazis. His portraits included people at the fringes of society, including gypsies and the unemployed. There was an official disapproval of his work. The Nazis banned his portraits because they did not glorify the ideal Aryan type, were too heterogeneous, and because they were suspicious of him because of one of his son's political affiliations. In 1936 they seized and destroyed some of his photographic plates and confiscated some of his negatives. He was able to salvage a quantity of them after the war, and reprinted a number of them. That same son, a member of a left wing socialist party, was arrested in 1934 and sentenced to ten years in prison. He died in prison in 1944, shortly before he was to be released.

Sander had moved to a rural area in 1942 to escape the Nazis, and he saved most of his negatives, but they were destroyed in a 1944 bombing raid of his studio. In 1946, after he returned to Cologne, 30,000 of his negatives were destroyed in an accidental fire. Nonetheless, approximately 1,800 of his portrait negatives for "People of the Twentieth Century" survived, as well as his notes and plans.

Walter was inspired by the realistic aspect of Sander's portraits, his photographic analysis of the subjects' characters and lifestyle and Sander's interest in his subjects' roles in society. Walter admired that the portraits showed sympathy for the human condition, but at the same time were unflattering in their realism and objectivity. Sander was pioneering in the idea of the archive as art, but Walter never tried to duplicate that effort.

Although Walter could have easily produced a comprehensive photographic document of the German people in Cologne, post war, from the 1950's to the 1990's, he chose not to retain his negatives. While much of Sander's work was destroyed by the Nazis, in bombing in the war, and by accidental fire, Walter destroyed his own. I have tried, continually, to analyze why Walter would do this, especially after he heard about Sander's grief from his loss of his negatives and prints. I wondered if it was that Walter did not value his own work, or if he did not value himself, or if he was so traumatized by what had happened to him, that most human and artistic endeavors seemed useless to him. Walter did not shed any more light on this issue, although I tried to broach the topic with him a number of times during the last month of his life. He did suffer acutely from post traumatic stress syndrome, which probably accounted for much of what he did or did not do. As his son, I wished that I could have preserved his legacy as August Sander's family did for him, in various exhibits and books.

Chapter Five

New York City in 1959

"Money's the cheapest thing.
Liberty and freedom is the most expensive."

"The best fashion show is definitely on the street.
Always has been and always will be."

"Legacy? I'm a worker in the factory; all we care about is today!
A legacy . . .what a bunch of baloney.

–Bill Cunningham, American Photographer

"Freaks was a thing I photographed a lot. . . . There's a quality of
legend about freaks. Like a person in a fairy tale who stops you
and demands that you answer a riddle. Most people go through
life dreading they'll have a traumatic experience. Freaks were
born with their trauma. They've already passed their test in life.
They're aristocrats."

"I work from awkwardness. By that I mean I don't like to arrange things. If I stand in front of something, instead of arranging it, I arrange myself."

–Diane Arbus, American Photographer

In 1959, when I was nine years old, Walter decided to return to New York City to see if he could make a go of it there, or to determine if he could emigrate to Brazil, where a few of his brothers lived and had developed a thriving business. He made the trip on his own. While he was in New York, he learned that his brothers did not want him to move to Brazil, and would not send any money for his passage. Their father had died, and the brothers had taken the father's money and did not leave any for Walter. Walter's plan then became to ascertain if he could set up a life in New York, and have us move there later. He never figured out a way for that to happen, as he was unable to get the proper visa. When I moved to New York in the 1970's, at least he was able to visit me, so his dream was partially realized.

Walter left Cologne and made the attempt to relocate during a three month period. I was not aware of the purpose of his trip at that time.

When he first arrived in New York, he went to a diner on the lower east side of Manhattan. He met a woman who was ten to fifteen years his senior. She was sitting near him, and overheard him tell the German waitress, in German, that he only had $1.75 and asked what he could eat for breakfast for that amount. The woman answered that she would pay for his breakfast, and that he should have whatever he wanted.

Walter was not ashamed of his inability to pay. He never felt guilty about not having money. He told the woman that he had just arrived from Germany, and he had no money and no prospects. He thanked her, and they started to talk. She was German too, but she was not a Jew. She had been married to a General in the German Army. Her husband did not want to stay in Germany after World War II as he thought he would be indicted, so he moved with her to New York to start a new life with two bags of money from the German Army. They were able to transfer the money to dollars, they bought a fancy apartment, and she lived like a queen. She claimed that her husband had been an administrator in the finance department of the German Army, and that he was not involved with the concentration camps and did not know what happened there until after he left Germany. He died in New York a few years later, and she remained a widow.

She asked Walter if he had a place to stay. He said no. She was lonely and told him he could have a bed in her apartment as she had several bedrooms. He went with her and brought his suitcase. After he went to sleep, in the middle of the night, she crept into his bed. They began a sexual relationship and he began to like it. After a week, his conscience started to hurt him. He felt that on some level he was sleeping with the enemy. He told her that he was married and had a child and a new baby back in Germany. She understood, and he left.

Walter contacted a close friend of his from Dachau Concentration Camp, Fred, who was gay, and lived in Greenwich Village. They were never lovers, just close friends. Fred was an executive at a large medical company. At that time, he was "in the closet at work," but not in his personal life. Fred had anglicized his name to assimilate into New York society. Walter stayed with him for the remainder of his trip, but Fred's apartment was small, so it was not a long-term plan.

There were no other old friends available to Walter in New York. Berenice Abbott had moved to Maine for health reasons. She was involved in a corporation she had founded called "House of Photography" with regard to her inventions, and had become involved with scientific photography. Thus, Walter did not get together with her at that time. Weegee was spending a lot of time in Hollywood working on filmmaking, and as an actor and a consultant, so he was unavailable also. Walker Evans worked for Time Inc., and they met a few times to take pictures together in the New York subways, but Walter was not the type who could work for an organization, nor could he get the necessary immigration papers to make his stay legal, so he did not try to pursue a job through Evan's connections.

Bill Cunningham

At that time, Fred was friendly with a man named Bill Cunningham, who later became a famous fashion photographer and contributed significantly to fashion journalism. Fred and Cunningham were both involved in the hidden gay scene in New York City. Cunningham was eleven years younger than Walter, but despite the age difference, their personalities clicked immediately. Cunningham was lanky with a ready smile, and was shy, humble, unassuming and amazingly creative. He had the eye of an artist, and the temperament of a kind, sweet priest. He was attracted to glitter, high society and celebrities. He was especially enamoured with the everyday person who made their appearance a visual show.

Cunningham never "came out" as a gay man. Walter was more outgoing, a "bad boy," a person attracted to the underworld, and had faced much harsher circumstances. He was probably more oriented toward sex with women than men, but was likely bisexual as he had relationships with men, too, throughout his life. Walter and Cunningham were attracted to the commonalities and differences in each other. Neither cared much about money for its own sake, and they wanted to lead a free, artistic life. They began to spend a lot of time together, rode bicycles all around Manhattan, and eventually had a brief affair.

Cunningham had a very different background than Walter, but they both had parents who disapproved of them, and were each on their own at an early age. Cunningham had been raised in Boston in a strict, Irish Catholic family. His family did not understand him, and fought his desire for an artistic life. He dropped out of Harvard University after two months, and moved to New York City at the age of nineteen. Soon after, he began to make hats, had his own business, and worked for a couture salon. In order to make money, he worked at a corner drugstore by day, in between making hats, and as a counterman at Howard Johnson's restaurant at night. He was able to eat because the jobs provided meals, and the tips paid for his millinery supplies.

Like Walter, he served in the Army, in Cunningham's case, in the Korean War. Cunningham never experienced the level of violence that Walter was subjected to, so, in some sense, he remained innocent. He was a spiritual person, and his background in and devotion to Catholicism and his proclivity toward homosexuality were always a battle for him. Walter did not believe in God, and had no problem with the fact that he enjoyed both men and women sexually. Walter was not repressed on any level. Cunningham felt liberated around Walter. Walter felt soothed by Cunningham's calm presence.

Walter told me some details about Cunningham's development as a photographer. His interest in photography began early. As a child, he photographed people at ski resorts and at parties. During World War II, he began to photograph people on the street using a little Brownie camera. Walter looked at some of his work, and thought he was a first-rate talent.

At the time Walter met him, Cunningham had a hat shop. He made the hats primarily for society women. Walter encouraged him to think about photography as a profession, and to become more involved in street photography so that he could take photographs of the people who truly interested him - everyday people, socialites, and fashion personalities. They spent hours on the street, observing people, taking photographs, and discussing the best angles and the most interesting subjects. Walter taught Cunningham what he had learned technically and aesthetically from Lee Miller, Weegee, Berenice Abbott, Walker Evans, Robert Capa and August Sander. They perused book stores together to look at photographs by these photographers and others.

Cunningham delighted in pointing out to Walter the fashions of the times worn by the most unusual women and men. He was most interested in people who put together outfits with their own creativity and panache. Walter never had any money to buy fancy clothes, but he had an innate sense of style, and looked like someone with flair. Cunningham, on the other hand, dressed during his leisure time in a uniform of black sneakers and a blue workman's jacket. Like Walter, he always carried a camera around his neck. Both of them preferred to be behind the camera rather than in front of it.

Cunningham showed Walter a different side of New York than Walter had experienced with Weegee and on his own forays into Time Square and other seedy areas. They would go through the back door to the fashionable theaters, hotels and restaurants, and observe the elegant women and their chic clothes. Cunningham lived with the philosophy that "those who seek beauty will find it." Cunningham thought that an appreciation of fashion might help Walter because, in his view, it was not frivolous, but was the "armor to survive the reality of everyday life." It was an important part of civilization to him.

Walter and Cunningham shared an acceptance of others, an essential optimism towards life, and an ability to have hope. Walter had faced harsher circumstances, so it was more difficult for him to be completely light hearted. Cunningham helped him to see beauty. They both loved people, and their favorite pastime together was people watching. They went to gay bars and parties together in New York and on Long Island. They both valued their independence, were originals, and liked to do things their own way.

Other than what he learned from Walter, Cunningham was a completely self-taught photographer. After Walter left New York, Cunningham improved his skills by taking candid photographs of fashion on the streets of New York. He was inspired by Walter's belief in his talent. In the 1960's he used an Olympus Pen-D half-frame camera which cost about $35.00. Later, in the 1970's, he became famous for his fashion photographs from the street and became a regular in the New York Times. He also took the first photographs of the gay community which were published in that newspaper. Eventually, he covered the visual fashion history of forty or fifty years in New York City.

I learned that many of Cunningham's photographs were never published and that he did not care because he did them for himself. None of Walter's photographs were ever published. He did them to live. Cunningham tried to be invisible when he took his photographs. Walter's personality is more apparent in those of his photographs which survived in that he posed many of his subjects. Their influence upon each other, nonetheless, was palpable. Cunningham let the street speak to him. For the most part, Walter arranged his subjects with his own vision.

Cunningham remained a lifelong friend of Walter. They attended Fred's funeral together when Fred died of AIDS, and every time Walter visited me in New York in the seventies, eighties and nineties, he always met up with Cunningham.

Diane Arbus

Although Walter appreciated Cunningham's touches of beauty and eccentricity, he was drawn more to the underbelly of society and to anti-glamour. While he appreciated viewing the belles of the ball, he was transfixed more intently by the "so-called social deviates." One day, while Walter was watching a three card monte game on the street in the Times Square area, he saw a petite woman with dark short hair in a pixie cut. She was walking around with a Nikon camera, taking photographs of all of the people that had mesmerized him. She had an elfin and fragile beauty.

Walter was never shy and started to speak with her. He was wearing his Leica on his wrist. It was clear that she needed a warm, compassionate ear, which he had, and they were interested in one another. They decided to go into a coffee shop for a conversation. Her name was Diane Arbus. Walter was struck by how intelligent and witty she was.

Arbus shared her early stories with him. She had been born in New York City to Jewish parents who owned a department store. She grew up with family wealth, and was raised by maids and governesses. She was "humiliated" by her wealth as a young person. Even though Walter was in dire financial circumstances at that moment, he understood how she needed to be free of class restraints. Her mother suffered from depression, and her father worked constantly. Her siblings and father were artistically inclined too.

Arbus had recently separated from her husband, whom she had married at the age of eighteen, and with whom she had two daughters. She was desperately unhappy that her marriage fell apart, and she deeply cared for him and for her children. In their early years together, they turned the bathroom of their apartment into a darkroom. Her husband had been a military photographer in World War II. They had a commercial photography business together although neither of them liked the fashion world. They took pictures for the top women's magazines and advertising agencies. She told Walter she knew of Cunningham's hats but did not know him. She was friendly with Richard Avedon, the fashion photographer, whose family also owned a department store.

In their business, her husband was the photographer and she was the art director and stylist, but she did not enjoy that role after a time. About two years prior, she had started out on her own with her photography. Her husband started taking acting classes and later became an actor. She and her husband continued to share a darkroom. His assistants developed her films, and she printed them.

She had begun a relationship with an art director and painter named Marvin, although he was married. Marvin encouraged her to create her first portfolio. Arbus shared that she was depressed and was somewhat at loose ends. She told Walter that she had terrible mood swings. Sometimes she was filled with energy and joy, breathless with excitement and ideas about what she could accomplish, and other times she was frightened by the things she thought she was eager for, sapped of energy and distraught.

They started off talking about their shared passion for photography. She told him that shortly after she married, she received her first camera, a Graflex, from her husband. She enrolled in photography classes with Berenice Abbott. They shared stories about Abbott and both respected her abilities.

Three years prior she had taken photography classes at the New School for Social Research in New York City from Lisette Model, who had been born in Vienna, Austria-Hungary and had emigrated to New York in 1938. Model was seventeen years older than Walter, and Arbus was five years younger than Walter. Model was Arbus's mentor, and remained her life long friend. Model believed that her father had molested her when she was young, and Arbus was a sympathetic ear. They shared many personal confidences. They were both traumatized in their own ways.

Model had become famous for her street photography in New York in the 1940's. Model's documentary photography emphasized average people in everyday situations, and their peculiarities. Arbus told Model that she wanted to photograph what was evil, meaning what was forbidden, what people were taught to "turn their backs on." These were human subjects who were too ugly, or frightening or dangerous to look at. Model emboldened her to do so.

When Walter met Arbus, she was pursuing her own projects, as Model had encouraged. She had the eye of a documentarian and an ability to find the personal, inner life of the subject. She used a 35mm Nikon camera. She would walk the streets, and meet her subjects, passersby, mostly by chance. Walter asked her where she took her photographs. She told him that she went everywhere with her camera. She walked the streets, went into the subway, to the circus, in dressing rooms, in the morgue, in movie theaters and diners, in grim apartments, in Central Park, on Coney Island and in New

Jersey homes. She said she worked hard to gain the trust of her subjects and befriended many of them. She even had sex with some of them. Some of her subjects included nudists, transvestites, midgets, drug-addicts and asylum inmates.

Arbus took photographs of odd-looking individuals on the outside of society. She became known as a photographer of "freaks," or, later, of everyday people whom Arbus made to look strange because, like Weegee, she used a flash. She also pointed her camera directly into the faces of her subjects as they looked into the camera. Critics said that her photographs were of "the quotidian and the extraordinary colliding." Walter talked about August Sander with her, and what he had accomplished with his portraits. Walter thought that both Sander and Arbus teased the viewer with their imaginations.

Arbus wanted the viewers to look at and acknowledge what they did not want to, and she pushed the boundaries of what was considered proper and tasteful. She called her photographs her butterfly collection. Walter could appreciate that goal, as he did the same thing in his photographs in Cologne. He took pictures of society's outcasts, including prostitutes, pimps and gypsies, as a reaction to the glorification by the Nazis of what they considered acceptable.

Arbus began photographing on assignment for magazines. She had not yet published her photographs in a Harper's Bazaar feature entitled "Portraits of Eccentrics" which initially launched Arbus's successful career. She took Walter to her darkroom, and apartment, and showed him many of her photographs, some of which later became famous. She felt herself, overall, to be a freak and someone with a morbid fascination with disturbing subjects.

Walter sensed that she was something of a voyeur in that she wanted to go places where she had never been as an escape from what she considered her boring, privileged origins. And yet, she did have a sense of empathy for her subjects. Perhaps she was drawn to the unsettling because she was unsettled. Maybe she was a humanist and compassionate. Walter was not certain if all or none of these observations applied. When looking at her photographs, Walter had the sense that some boundary had been crossed between the photographer and subject, and that in viewing them himself, he was implicated in it. It was as if her photographs were looking back at him.

Walter and Arbus were both bohemians and risk takers in life and in their art. They both took "naughty" photographs. Arbus took Walter to Coney Island, and to Hubert's Museum in Times Square, next door to the Amsterdam Theater on West 42nd Street, where they had all manner of freaks. Both she and Walter took photographs of a bearded lady with a thirteen-inch beard, a woman with elephant skin, a man with a deformed face, a sword swallower, a snake dancer, a human caterpillar, and a flea circus. They took pictures together of wax museums, dance halls and flophouses. They could not get enough of what they were seeing, or of one another. At that time, she used her 35-millimeter camera with natural lighting and liked grainy textures. Walter used his Leica and preferred more precise, sharper images.

Walter never became attached to his subjects. He cajoled and hypnotized them in his way, but then he was finished. Arbus, on the other hand, became mesmerized with her subjects, and they of her, such that her images had a deep, psychological dimension. Once Arbus had permission to photograph some of her subjects, she spent hours, even days, taking more and more photographs of them. Both she and Walter were very direct and open, and people responded to that.

Both Arbus and Walter wanted others to see people who were outcasts as within the range of normal human behavior. They thought of themselves, in some sense, as outcasts. They did not view their subjects as objects, but as people to befriend. Arbus took it a bit further with her psychological intensity. They both had huge hearts and felt connected to people in their own ways. The biggest difference between them was that Arbus was ambitious for her art, and Walter did not take his art seriously that way.

Arbus confided many of her deepest thoughts to Walter. She told Walter that she feared some of her sexual urges, not only toward her subjects, but she had also started to experiment with group sex and could not get enough of it. She admitted to him that she had a long-term incestuous relationship with her brother, who was a poet. She was having an affair with a married man. Walter did not judge any of her behavior, as he had experimented sexually throughout his life. Perhaps, as artists, a common trait was to live outside of societal norms. The rules were not for them. Walter was able to do things without guilt, while it seemed that she did have guilt but it did not guide her behavior. Her sexual relations had a compulsive quality.

Walter was living with his gay friend, Fred, and Arbus was living in a carriage house in Greenwich Village with her two daughters. It was not easy to carry on an affair. A number of times they went to a seedy hotel in Times Square to have sex after a day of photographing. She lost herself for a time, but after the sex they often spoke about her feeling that she had problems with her chemistry, and that she sometimes felt suicidal. Walter had post traumatic stress disorder but not depression. He too had considered suicide while he was in the concentration camp, while he was homeless in Israel, and after returning to Cologne and living amongst Nazi families. He told her that he had decided that life was too interesting. He was curious to see what would happen next. Arbus hoped that she would eventually feel the same way. When Walter learned that she had committed suicide twelve years later he was deeply moved, but not surprised. She experienced everything more powerfully than he did.

Walter returned to Cologne because he could not get a visa to stay longer in New York. Germany was the only real home he had ever known, but it was not an entirely hospitable one. He missed our family, and felt that he had not achieved his goal of bringing us all to the United States, but was resigned to the fact that we would have to remain in Germany. I remember thinking, at some later point, that I was going to be the one to escape, and everyone would visit me in New York.

Chapter Six

Back in Germany: Photography, Gambling, Sex, Art, and Confinement in a Mental Institution

"Part of the $10 million I spent on gambling, part on booze and part on women. The rest I spent foolishly."

–George Raft, American Actor

"Art is the only power to free humankind from all repression."

"This is why we believe that a well-ordered idea of ecology and professionalism can stem only from art – art in the sense of the sole, revolutionary force, capable of transforming the earth, humanity, the social order etc...Art is, then, a genuinely human medium for revolutionary change in the sense of completing the transformation from a sick world to a healthy one. In my opinion only art is capable of doing it."

–Joseph Beuys, German Artist, Art Theorist, and Pedagogue

Photography, Gambling and Sex

After Walter returned to Cologne from New York, he started up his photography business again, and returned to his old employment venues. He continued to use August Sander's business for his developing and printing. He continued to go to the Photokina picture shows at the trade fair. August Sander's photographs had been exhibited at Photokina in 1951 when Walter was living in Israel. Sander reminded him about the possibility of exhibiting there, and tried to encourage him to think about expanding his photographic horizons.

After his sojourn in New York, Walter became even more friendly with one of the organizers of Photokina, who also founded the German Society of Photography, L. Fritz Gruber. Gruber was sympathetic toward what Walter had endured as a Jew. Gruber was a co-founder and co-publisher of weekly newspapers in Cologne in 1930, which were against National Socialism (the Nazis - the National Socialist German Workers' Party). In 1933, the Nazis banned his newspapers, and Gruber was forced to emigrate to London. He finally returned back to Cologne in 1949.

Gruber tried to interest Walter in joining photography societies and groups, and in exhibiting his photographs, but Walter was not interested in doing so. Gruber, in his effort to inspire him, talked to Walter about Man Ray, who was an American visual artist who spent most of his career in Paris. He showed him some of Man Ray's photographs as he was known for his photography as well as his surrealist paintings.

Gruber had met Man Ray in Paris in 1956, and they had a twenty year collaboration with one another. In 1960, Gruber dedicated a solo exhibition to Man Ray in Cologne, and he published a book about his portraits in 1963. Walter was interested in Man Ray's background as his parents were Jewish immigrants from Russia, and he grew up in Brooklyn, New York. His birth name was Emmanuel Radnitzky. Walter was impressed with his artistry and his contributions to the Dada and Surrealist movements. Lee Miller and Berenice Abbott had both worked with him and had shared their stories about him with Walter.

Walter was not motivated to try to succeed and to become recognized and admired for his photography, or for anything else. He wanted total freedom from deadlines and responsibilities and from the pressure of living up to other people's expectations. He wanted to make enough money so that he could go off and pleasure himself with it. He never cared what other people thought of him, and would not derive any ego gratification from being lauded as a photographer. Eventually Gruber and Sander gave up on trying to get him to become more involved in photography in a public way, beyond what he did for clients.

In addition to his devotion to his family, what drew Walter's attention most intently during the sixties and seventies were his carnal and gambling interests. Gambling was illegal in Germany in the 1950's to the 1970's. Walter would have to go to back alley rooms to participate. Perhaps gambling decreased his ambition for photography, if he even had the ambition in the first place. He looked for the parties and the good times. If someone wanted to go out for a beer, he would get out of bed and go, no matter the time. If someone wanted to have sex, or if he had the urge and opportunity, he would usually do it. If there was gambling going on, he would find a way to be involved. He followed the feeling of the moment, and if he would get a charge out of doing it, he would. He still believed he was entitled because when he was in his twenties, he had lived eighty years based upon what happened to him. He determined that the rest of his life he would dedicate himself to experiencing life's thrills as he defined them.

In the 1960's, as part of the health system in Germany, he went to a spa every two years. Sometimes he went with my mother, and sometimes he went alone. When he went alone, he usually had an affair. It was common for people to have affairs at the spa. They called the person they met at a spa a "kurschatten," which translates to "spa shadow." The relationship during that time was not supposed to be a commitment or mean anything beyond sex.

One time he had an affair at a spa with a very young woman when he was in his forties. She was extremely unstable. Some months after he returned from the spa, he was contacted by the family of the young woman, who blamed him for her suicide. They found letters of hers after her death which mentioned the affair. My father said that he felt badly about what happened to her, but he did not believe that he was the cause of her suicide and did not feel guilt about it. He was not embarrassed about the incident when my mother found out.

I asked my father if he was addicted to sex. He said no. He said he just liked to have it with more people than just with my mother, and he had only occasional flings. When I asked him about his longer standing affairs, he said that those relationships were just for sex and there was no emotional attachment on his part. For his own part, he did not believe that monogamy was possible. Maybe for others, but not for him.

I asked my father if he thought he was addicted to gambling. He admitted it freely. He acknowledged that he was not able to regulate it, and that he spent more time and money gambling than he intended. He was in it for the short term pleasure it brought him.

He told me that the only time he felt calm was when all the money was gone and he could not gamble anymore. His gambling had a compulsive quality to it the way that sex did for Diane Arbus as she had described it to him. He never thought of giving it up, even with the negative consequences and despite his love for our family. It was his life crutch. Gambling was his reward for his post traumatic stress.

When my father went gambling, he said it was like being in a bubble. He lost all track of time. When he lost, he chased his losses, and when he won, he could not walk away. It was not about winning, but about the play time. He said that once he started gambling, he could not stop until he ran out of money or the gambling place closed. All his energy and focus was heightened and in the game. His brain did not guide him to better choices, and he did not know why he did it. There was an all consuming nature to it, and will power to stop did not come into it at all. He was incapable of delaying his gratification. He needed to seek the thrill he got from gambling, while simultaneously numbing his pain and escaping.

I asked him if he thought about the fact that with the money lost, there would not be enough to pay for rent and bills or buy food. He said no. He said that gambling for him was the only place he felt himself, and winning meant more time to do it. It helped him to cope, to relax, and to feel like a winner. It helped him to escape his problems with his dark memories. It was a counterbalance to his lack of motivation, his sleeping too much, and his low energy. Being in the action made him feel as if he were in his own skin, and he experienced a kind of high from it. Even watching others gamble, like observing the three card monte games in New York, gave him a secondary gambling high.

We talked about his not wanting to grow up and be reliable, and his needing a lot of "me time." It is not unusual for gamblers to work for themselves, and to gamble alone. He recalled that he had been involved in gambling since he was a teenager, and that his decisions were usually impulsive in nature.

He did not like to plan in advance. He said he always thought that things would work out and he relied on the inspiration of the moment to guide him. He felt alive and capable when he gambled, even when he ended up sleeping on the street or a park bench because he did not have enough money to get back home.

He was grateful to my mother for putting up with him and for centering the universe around him. He knew that was so. If he wanted a special meal, or an ingredient for a dish they did not have, my mother would take care of it for him, even if it meant travelling miles to get it. He enjoyed simple pleasures in addition to his gambling. Staying in bed, reading, walking, and trying new foods were all exquisite fulfillments for him. He was addicted to chaos, but he also drew inspiration from the moment. For him, gambling had not ruined his life.

My mother ran the household, and he benefited from having that structure. She tried to get as much control as she could over the money so that Walter would not spend it all, and, to his credit, he did not interfere with that too much. She was truly his helper. He remembered being homeless, and he never felt it was that far away from happening again, but he did not fear it.

It was as if he led a second life which had nothing to do with us, but we stuck by him despite it all. He was fortunate that he never lost everything. He never felt suicidal from his gambling. Even at the time of his death he had the love of his family and friends. His gambling never stripped him of being fun, loving, and generous when he was available, which were the best parts of him, and kept him connected. In that sense, he was lucky. We were fortunate, too, because his gambling and sexual escapades did not ruin our family.

Joseph Beuys

My father was intellectually interested as well. Although he did not want to make his own artistry known to the public, he was attracted to the artists of his time and to the ideas they generated. He had many ideas of his own, but shared them solely with his friends and family. In the 1960's, Walter came into contact with one artist who changed the way he looked at things. His name was Joseph Beuys. Beuys, in his lifetime, was a performance artist, painter, sculptor, installation artist, graphic artist, art theorist, and pedagogue. He was a philosopher, whose work was based upon concepts of humanism, social philosophy and anthroposophy (a system established by the Austrian philosopher, Rudolf Steiner, to optimize physical and mental health), and a political activist.

In 1964 and 1965, my father traveled on numerous occasions to the City of Dusseldorf, Germany, which was only a forty minute car ride from Cologne. There was a trial being conducted against eleven SS camp personnel who worked at the Treblinka extermination camp, and he wanted to listen to the testimony of many of the witnesses. Walter felt immensely gratified that these individuals were being brought to justice, although they represented only a small number of SS personnel who participated in the extermination of the Jews brought to Treblinka. Eventually the accused were convicted, and many received life imprisonment and long sentences. However, in actuality, most served very few years.

At one of the trial days, Joseph Beuys was also in attendance, as a protest against the Nazis. He was three years younger than Walter, had a boyish look, and was wearing a fedora hat and a vest, which was his signature style. Walter struck up a conversation with him in the hallway of the courthouse.

Walter recognized him from articles he had read in the newspaper about his performance art. Beuys had a charismatic presence which intrigued Walter. Beuys found Walter to be charming, intelligent and engaging.

Beuys was very open with him. He shared with Walter that he was a member of the Hitler Youth in 1936, and that he participated in the Nuremberg rally when he was fifteen years old. He also told him that in 1941 he had volunteered for the Luftwaffe, which was the aerial warfare branch of the German military. He said that in 1944, as a member of a bomber unit, his plane crashed on the Crimean Front, and he was rescued from the crash. After that, he was deployed to the Western Front and he was wounded in action more than five times. After serving time in a British internment camp after the German surrender in 1945, he was released, and went back to his parents in Germany.

After the war, he studied art, and, in an attempt to recuperate and to heal himself, he made hundreds of drawings and sculptures. He spent a decade making art in solitude. Beuys shared with Walter that he felt a terrible sense of guilt about supporting the Nazi war effort, and that in the 1950's, he went through a period of a deep depression, and questioned everything in his life. In an attempt to expiate his "sins" he had submitted a design in an international competition for an Auschwitz-Birkenau Concentration Camp memorial, but he did not win. Beuys felt that he would always have trouble reconciling his involvement in World War II and would have to spend the rest of his life trying to make peace with it.

Walter understood his need to heal himself and to help to heal society. He and Beuys decided to meet whenever Walter came to Dusseldorf. They felt that by talking with one another, they might make some progress with their own demons. They acknowledged that their relationship was a step toward making the world a more humane place, a German and a German Jew together who had fought against each other in World War II. Those discussions went on until Beuys died in 1986.

At the time they met, Beuys was a professor of "monumental sculpture" at the Kunstakademie Dusseldorf. Walter respected his social philosophical ideas. He had abolished entry requirements into his class, which was opposed by the institution. Walter supported Beuys and thought that his action exemplified an important democratic principle. Beuys was eventually dismissed from his post because of it. Nonetheless, he persisted in giving public lectures and participating in public discussions throughout his life, and in the 1980's became a visiting professor.

Beuys invited Walter to many of his performances. Walter read about one of his first performances which was conducted in 1964 at the Technical College Aachen, west of Cologne. Beuys had created a performance as part of a festival of new art which coincided with the twentieth anniversary of an assassination attempt on Adolf Hitler. A group of students interrupted his performance. One of the students punched Beuys in the face, and the newspapers printed a photograph of him with his nose bloodied and his arm raised, which Walter saw. Walter told Beuys that he was extremely upset about the incident as it brought up old wounds for him. For Beuys, it was life affirming as he was supporting something he believed in, even if it resulted in a bloody nose, whereas his own war efforts were a source of humiliation, pain and suffering.

In 1965, Walter attended his performance entitled "How to Explain Pictures to a Dead Hare." That effort was part of Beuys's teaching of philosophy, and showed his emphasis on the importance of intellectual exchange. For Beuys, the performance exemplified, also, the difficulty of explaining things. The audience looked through the gallery window, and saw Beuys with his face covered in honey and gold leaf. He had an iron slab attached to his boot. The audience watched him cradling a dead hare and making muffled noises into the hare's ear, as well as explaining the drawings to the hare, which were up on the walls. Walter thought the performance was odd, but somehow deeply moving.

Many times he told Walter that "teaching is my greatest work of art." He explained to Walter that he saw his role as an artist as a teacher or shaman "who could guide society in a new direction." Beuys believed that art should be democratic and that there should be a "collapsing of the space between life and art." Walter told Beuys that photography could be viewed as one medium which accelerated that process.

When Walter told Beuys that he did not think of himself as an artist, Beuys argued with him. He said that everyone is an artist, and that Walter had discovered the creativity in everyday life and he had used it in his photography. He felt that Walter was in touch with his invisible energies and that he was using his emotions and his thinking for his creativity. Walter understood Beuys's idea that art was educative as well as therapeutic, as Walter's photography had been therapeutic on some level for him, and for his subjects.

Walter and Beuys discussed New York and the art scene there many times. Walter did not return to visit New York until 1975. Thus, he missed Beuys' performance art in New York in 1974 called "I Like America and America Likes Me," a symbolic event. Beuys described it to him.

Beuys was taken by ambulance from the airport to the gallery space where he did the performance. He was in a room with a coyote for eight hours over a three-day period. The performance went from symbolic elements to what was required by the realities of the situation. At the end of the three days, he hugged the coyote and was taken back to the airport in an ambulance. He saw nothing of America other than the coyote.

He told Walter he wanted to isolate and insulate himself, and to have it be all about him and the coyote. It was a dialogue with the animal, where he, as a healer, or shaman, would enact a "symbolic reconciliation between modern American society, the natural world, and Native American culture." Conceptual art was fascinating for Walter, and opened him up to new ideas, but he did not want to do performance art himself because he preferred his perch behind the camera.

Politically, Beuys became a pacifist, and spent years opposing nuclear weapons, concentrating on environmental causes, and seeking educational reform. He founded or co-founded many political organizations including the German Student Party, the Free International University, and the German Green Party. He even ran for political office. Walter did not become politically involved, but was a sounding board for his ideas.

Beuys believed that art could bring about revolutionary change, and that society as a whole should be looked at as one great work of art to which every person can contribute creatively. He truly believed in his utopian vision that the world could be more peaceful, democratic and creative. Walter felt enlivened by these thoughts, as he desperately wanted to believe that a better world was possible. His conversations with Beuys reminded him of the intellectual discussions he had in Dachau Concentration Camp with political activists there, although Beuys had an added spiritual dimension to his theories.

His most famous "social sculpture," a cooperative effort toward positive change, was called 7000 Oaks. Seven thousand trees were planted throughout Germany, mostly in areas that had been destroyed during the bombings in World War II, as a major reforestation project. This idea was replicated in the United States in Minneapolis and other places. It reminded Walter of the efforts by the Jewish National Fund and other organizations to plant trees in Israel. In fact, Walter recalled that the holiday of Tu Bishvat in the Jewish religion was connected with the planting of trees in Israel, which had been going on for centuries. Walter never heard anybody making the connection between what Beuys did and what the Jews did in Palestine and Israel. But, he reasoned, a good idea is a good idea.

Both Walter and Beuys embellished stories and made up some things about themselves when they presented themselves to other people. Walter, however, was truthful about his wartime experiences. Some said that Beuys was not and made up the myth that when his plane crashed on the Crimean front during World War II, he was rescued by nomadic Tatar tribesmen who nursed him back to health by wrapping him in animal fat and felt, which elements later figured in his art pieces. Beuys used myth and real and imagined elements in his art. Walter used other means of escape. They were each trying to heal in their own ways, and they both struggled.

Walter in a Mental Institution

In the early 1970's, in Germany, Walter had to be re-evaluated in a mental institution for his post traumatic stress to determine his level of disability. His struggle was ongoing. He spent a month there, after which it was determined that he was one hundred percent disabled. Walter told me that he faked his psychiatric illness so that he would be entitled to a higher payment from the government, but I suspect that was only partially true. We knew he had a crisis of the soul even though he behaved in an upbeat manner and as a jokester around his family and friends. For the psychiatrists he pretended he was sicker, and for us he pretended he was more balanced.

I visited Walter at the psychiatric hospital with my mother and brother. On his ward, he was surrounded by people who were talking to themselves, or catatonic and not speaking at all. Many screamed or writhed on the floor, their eyes were vacant, and their faces were contorted. Some were wearing straight jackets. He told us the staff could be brutal sometimes. They treated the patients with infantilizing condescension, sometimes beat them, mostly ignored them, and often left them in their own feces for lengthy periods. The walls were green and the hallways institutional. The rooms for the patients were stark, and there were mostly four or five people to a room. The common room had no pictures on the walls, no carpet, and no homey touches whatsoever. The administration did not want to have objects that the patients could throw around. The lighting throughout was eerie, and there were few windows with natural light.

It was a scary place, but for Walter, it was not nearly as frightening as the concentration camp had been. This experience was summer camp from his perspective. The food was edible and he ate three meals. He had a clean bed and clean sheets. He was allowed to take a shower regularly. He was given clean hospital gowns to wear. There were toilets and sinks. If he kept quiet and followed the rules, nobody beat him. The ward was not overcrowded because so many of the mentally ill had been exterminated by the Nazis during their ethnic cleansing. He joked with the staff and with those patients who were responsive, so he was well liked and given privileges. That was the good news.

We brought him his Leica camera so that he had something to do to fill up the hours. The staff allowed him to have it there as long as he did not abuse it. He slept with the Leica around his neck as he was afraid it would be stolen or broken. I have that camera in my safe now for the same reasons. It is my primary object to remember him by.

He took many photographs of the other patients and staff. Sometimes he asked permission to take the pictures, and some of them he took surreptitiously. The photographs rivaled anything that Diane Arbus had taken in their compassion and poignancy. Some of them were as stark in their realism as a Weegee crime photograph, or an August Sander portrait of a laborer. He took some self-portraits which showed his loneliness while there. The photography seemed to be integral to his recovery and a respite from his loneliness. He also used the camera to connect with the others there, both patients and staff, and as a vehicle to humanize the experience.

Not surprisingly, he became worse while he was institutionalized. My mother made every attempt to get him released. The truth of his life was that he had been subjected to brutality by insane people in the concentration camp; that he had been subjected to an insane world when he was released with more war, dislocation, and dysfunction; and then he was being told he was the crazy one. While he wanted it to be true for the money, he knew he was a sensitive soul who had survived every imaginable horror nonetheless. He knew that most of the staff at that hospital could never have endured what he did, not even for a minute. For him it was a game, but it had consequences. Unlike Beuys, he could not turn his experiences into art or hope. He just worked on surviving each day. Some days were better than others. If he could find amusement and pleasure, he would follow the source.

Chapter Seven

Visiting New York in the 1970's

"For me the camera is a sketch book, an instrument of intuition and spontaneity, the master of the instant which, in visual terms, questions and decides simultaneously. It is by economy of means that one arrives at simplicity of expression."

–Henri Cartier-Bresson, a French Humanist
Photographer, Pioneer of Street Photography, Filmmaker,
and a Co-Founding Member of Magnum Photos

"I felt that the camera grew an extension of my eyes and moved with me."

–Ilse Bing, a German Avant-Garde and
Commercial Photographer

"What will obviously make the difference between a successful and an unsuccessful photographer is the intellectual 'baggage' he brings with him. He should have a heightened sense of curiosity

and be able to foresee and predict certain sequences very quickly. I think the old-fashioned statement 'f/8 and be there!' is true even today. The ability of the photographer to 'get in' to shoot is 99 percent of the battle and requires that he be 'trusted'."

–Cornell Capa, Hungarian American Photographer, Member of Magnum Photos, Photo Curator, and the Younger Brother of Photo-journalist and War Photographer Robert Capa

"The photograph should be more interesting or more beautiful than what was photographed."

–Garry Winogrand, American Street Photographer

From 1975 on, my father visited me each year in New York. My mother would accompany him most of the time. I had emigrated to New York from Germany, and was employed as a journalist. Not surprisingly, one of my permanent assignments was to cover photographers and artists, which included articles on their exhibits, books, performances and lives.

Walter's heart, or demons, however you want to look at it, drove him to spend most of his time in the Times Square area or on buses to gambling areas. He was most comfortable with street people, eccentric individuals, and those with vices. He was not open about much of what he did with these people. I do know that he found conventional people leading routine lives boring.

He was curious about all artistic people, especially photographers who had become famous for their work, and he wanted to meet some of them. New York was certainly the place for that to happen. I told him where he might find people, procured invitations to openings for him, and he pursued meetings on his own while I was working. Sometimes I took him along when I conducted interviews. My mother preferred to stay in my apartment most of the time, cooking, entertaining relatives, and reading.

As you are reading the following accounts of the meetings between Walter and these famous people, you will notice that his personality and story recedes into the background, and their stories come to the fore. That is not an accident as what Walter was most known for during that time in his life was his warmth, and his ability to listen intelligently. During the seventies, eighties and nineties, Walter lived life fully in his own way, continued to take photographs to make a living, but did not have drive and ambition beyond a simple life. The reason for his approach is probably the result of his personality and age.

Most of these other photographers wanted their work to become known, courted public opinion, became famous, and engaged more in society. Walter was curious about what they did and how they did it, but he was passive when it came to applying their lessons to his own life. Their successes did not necessarily make them happier than Walter was. Perhaps it is my personal frustration as his son that the world did not get the opportunity to appreciate his work.

Henri Cartier-Bresson

In 1975, I heard through the art grapevine that Henri Cartier-Bresson was in New York City for an exhibition of his drawings at the Carlton Gallery. I told Walter about the opening of the exhibition, and he attended it.

At the exhibition Walter began a conversation with Cartier-Bresson, who was ten years older than Walter. Walter was wearing his Leica camera around his neck, and they started to speak about that. At the time of the exhibition, Cartier-Bresson had ceased his active working relationship with Magnum photos, a cooperative of photographers. He had turned from photography to drawing and painting.

Walter had admired his photographs for decades. He heard stories about him from Lee Miller, Berenice Abbott, and Robert Capa. Walter told Cartier-Bresson about his own relationship with Robert Capa in Israel. Walker Evans had told Walter that he had exhibited with Cartier-Bresson in 1935 at the Julien Levy Gallery in New York and they talked about that exhibit. Cartier-Bresson shared with him that he no longer liked to give interviews and talk about his prior career as a photographer, but he still found it stimulating to exchange thoughts with fellow photographers.

Cartier-Bresson's wife was not with him on the trip, so he agreed to have Walter escort him around New York City the next day. Walter sold himself as a tour guide and fellow artist. As they meandered throughout the City, Walter learned more about him as they discussed their lives. Cartier-Bresson was born into a wealthy family in France in 1908. His father made his fortune as a textile manufacturer. He was similar to Walter in that during his teenage years, he rebelled against his parents and became interested in communism, although art was his main passion. He studied painting, and became part of the Parisian avant-garde in the late 1920's. He did not want to go into the family business, but he did benefit from their financial support for his artistic endeavors. Walter recalled that he did not have any financial support.

Cartier-Bresson remembered that when he was in his early twenties, he received a gift of a simple Brownie camera, and began to experiment with it. He purchased his first 35mm Leica shortly afterwards. Cartier-Bresson acknowledged that his photographs show the influence of his exposure to Cubism and Surrealism. He tried to employ the Surrealists' technique of using the subconscious in his work, and to "reconfigure the usual and the unusual." In addition, he was attracted to the subject of outcasts, as Walter was. He told Walter that he was especially influenced by the photographers Man Ray and Eugene Atget.

He then became a photojournalist in the 1930's and traveled the world with his 35mm Leica camera. He experimented with street photography. He also experimented with film and became an assistant to Jean Renoir, the French filmmaker, for three years. Cartier-Bresson was drawn to films involving stories about real life, and he made his own documentary in 1937. He told Walter that he did not believe that he was a good filmmaker.

He started to recall his personal relationships at that time. He had an open sexual relationship with a close friend's wife, with the friend's approval, as part of the sexual expressiveness of the times. Tragically, the friend committed suicide and Cartier-Bresson's affair with his wife ended several years later. They talked about how difficult it can be to have love relationships, and how much pain can be attached to it. He married a Javanese dancer in 1937, and they lived in a servants' flat in Paris where he used the bathroom to develop the film.

Similar to Walter, his approach to photography remained simple, and the same, throughout his career. Their discussion included the technical aspects of Leica cameras, a subject which Walter preferred, always, to delve into, as they both used Leicas. They both did not use artificial light, dark room effects or cropping. They both used light equipment loads. Walter used a 35mm lens, and Cartier-Bresson used a 50mm lens, and sometimes a 90mm lens. They both did their edits through the viewfinder while taking the photograph. They both worked in black and white. They both had a "good eye," and a warm heart. Because Cartier-Bresson often took stealth photographs, he wrapped black tape around the camera's chrome body so that people would be less likely to detect that he was taking photographs. Sometimes he would hide the camera under a handkerchief. More of Walter's work was posed. Cartier-Bresson developed a unique way to combine his content and form. Walter had his own style.

They shared their traumatic war time experiences. After the German invasion of France in 1940, Cartier-Bresson was drafted into the French army, into the film and photography unit. He was captured by the Germans, and spent three years in a prisoner-of-war camp run by the Nazis. He managed to escape, after several unsuccessful attempts, which had landed him in solitary confinement. He joined the French Resistance, and continued with his film work, photography and coverage of World War II and its aftermath. He had buried his Leica camera in farmland in France, which he then recovered, and continued to use.

In 1943, he made a series of portraits of artists, which included Matisse, Bonnard and Braque. Walter was impressed with how many important people he had access to at that time. He told Walter an amusing story. In 1946, he was thought to have been killed in the war, and he helped in the preparation of a so-called posthumous show of his work at the Museum of Modern Art in New York. The next year, he founded the Magnum photo agency with Robert Capa and others. It was a cooperative picture agency owned by its members. It was an unusual concept in that the photographers owned the rights to their photographs. He spent the next twenty years on assignment all over the world.

While he was traveling east after the war, he photographed Mahatma Gandhi in early 1948, shortly before his assassination. Cartier-Bresson had enormous respect for Gandhi which shined through in his photographs. He documented events after Gandhi's death and its impact on India, which were in Life Magazine and became famous. Walter was familiar with those photographs.

After his three-year odyssey throughout Asia, Cartier-Bresson returned to France and published his first book in 1952 entitled "The Decisive Moment," which was a collection of 126 of his photographs from the East and West. The cover was illustrated by Matisse. Walter told him that he was impressed with that book as it showed what Walter sometimes tried to achieve, the capture of a candid moment. Cartier-Bresson said that the art world liked to use his quote that summed up his philosophy: "To me, photography is the simultaneous recognition, in a fraction of a second, of the significance of an event as well as of a precise organization of forms which gave that event its proper expression." Walter felt confident that he knew when he saw a good composition, and that he had the intuition to know when to click the camera. In that sense he was empowered by his creativity, but never gave himself enough credit.

Cartier-Bresson told Walter that he continued to travel around the world over the next twenty years and to document "triumphs and tragedies," and the human response to defining moments of history. Walter respected his use of photography in the service of humanity, and his deep regard for people which was evident in his photographs. Often, Cartier-Bresson photographed the reaction of the crowd of people rather than the event itself. Weegee used that technique too, and Walter had experimented with that.

Over the course of his career, Cartier-Bresson had covered such notable events as the Spanish Civil War, the Chinese revolution, Khrushchev's Russia, George VI's coronation, the Berlin Wall, the deserts of Egypt and much more. He had other books published including books about China, the Europeans and the people of Moscow, and the face of Asia. He photographed famous people. He took pictures of ordinary life. Walter told him that he was in awe of the way in which he captured decisive moments of human life around the world.

Walter asked him how he felt about having received so many awards and retrospectives for his photography throughout the years. He told Walter that it fed his ego but not his soul. He just wanted to be alone with his drawings and paintings. He had destroyed his early paintings from the 1920's because he could not achieve what he wanted to. Now he was trying, anew, to express himself with that medium, but he was finding it more challenging. With photography, his eye, head and heart aligned in an intuitive way.

They shared stories about their family lives. Walter told him he was still in love with and lived with the same woman he married in 1949, but that he often felt the need to stray sexually. He talked about me and my brother, and our interest in the arts. My brother had become an architect.

Cartier-Bresson told Walter that in 1967 he was divorced from his first wife of thirty years. They never had children. The next year he returned to his painting and drawing and began to retreat from photography. In 1979 he married a Belgian photographer who was thirty years younger than he, and they had a daughter together. He was happy in his marriage. He did not share with Walter why he started a new life in his later years. Cartier-Bresson had a shyness about him, and did not like to dig too deeply into his own emotional life. He did share with Walter that his personality was shaped by his wartime experiences hiding from the Nazis during World War II, and that, despite his fame, he had shied away from publicity, and did not want his face to be recognized on the street. That anonymity had helped him with his photography. It also influenced his wanting to keep his private life private.

To Walter's dismay, Cartier-Bresson described himself as having no imagination, and having been a failed painter and filmmaker. He told Walter, also, that he did not believe that his photographs were art, but just his gut reaction to fleeting situations that he came upon. Walter told him that he agreed that photographs were not art, but Walter had retreated into the private realm with his work to such an extent that the world never was able to judge for itself if Walter's photographs were, in fact, art. That debate seems irrelevant in today's world in that photography has been fully accepted as an art form.

Of all the photographers Walter met, he was particularly impressed by the work and life of Cartier-Bresson. He took magnificent photographs and yet remained humble, he was brave and daring to place himself in harm's way throughout the world to capture moments in history for the benefit of the rest of humanity, and he helped to lead an organization to help fellow photographers maintain their autonomy. And, despite his struggles with painting, he pursued that form of expression again in later life. He continued to challenge himself.

Ilse Bing

In 1976, Walter arrived in New York City for his yearly visit to me. I wanted to keep him occupied with activities other than gambling. The German-born Jewish photographer, Ilse Bing, was in town for a retrospective solo exhibition of her work at the Lee Witkin Gallery. She had recently been included in an exhibition at the Museum of Modern Art as well. Walter was enthusiastic about attending the opening. Cartier-Bresson had mentioned to Walter that he was in Paris with Bing in the 1930's, that they had been in the same artistic and social milieu along with Man Ray, and that she had influenced many photographers then, and now. I encouraged Walter to take part in it.

Walter was about nineteen years younger than Bing, but he had heard much about her because she was famous for using a 35 mm Leica camera, and for her street photographs, scenes of urban architecture, still lifes, self portraits, portraits, adver-tisements and commissioned photo essays. A critic had called her "Queen of the Leica." Walter never used any other camera, and he was looking forward to talking with her about the Leica as she was such an early user and experimenter with it. Walter was familiar with her iconic "Self-Portrait with Leica," from 1931.

In the only photographs Walter had ever seen of her, she had dark hair, big, penetrating eyes with a slight dark shadow under them, and pencil thin eyebrows. When he arrived at the opening, he saw a woman with gray hair, bangs, and the same mesmerizing eyes he saw in the photographs of her. When he introduced himself, Walter was extremely charming toward her. She appreciated a younger man bestowing her with atten-tion and flattery. They agreed to meet at a German restaurant in New York City, to have Wiener Schnitzel, and other traditional German fare, and to share stories.

When they met at the restaurant the following week, Bing shared her account of some important memories from her past. They developed the instant rapport of two people who were eternally in search of a home. Here is what she told him. She had been born in Frankfurt, Germany to a wealthy Jewish family. Similar to Walter's family, they were not religious Jews. Unlike Walter, however, because she was older than him, she went to school before the Nazis came to power, so she was able to become highly educated. Walter was envious of that opportunity.

She studied the arts, music, and later mathematics and physics in University, but then turned to art history when she moved to Vienna. In 1924, she began a doctoral program studying architecture, and she took photographs of buildings for use in her dissertation. She was fascinated by the technical aspects of photography, as well as by art, and she was excited about the possibility of combining her two interests into one passion.

In 1929, she bought a Leica, and determined that she would move to Paris the next year to work on photography as a freelance photojournalist, which work she had already begun in Frankfurt. She had been a photojournalist for a German illustrated magazine supplement called Das Illustrierte Blatt. Her family and friends did not approve of her abandoning her academic career, but she was determined. They felt that her working for such a magazine was menial work and beneath her. She told Walter that she did not choose photography, that it chose her. She went along with the trend of the time, which was when mechanical devices "penetrated into the field of art." For Bing, there was no question that photography was art, although that thinking was a source of debate at that time.

After she moved to Paris, she became part of the avant-garde and surrealist scene. She embraced the creative life there which included exhibitions, journals and performances. For the next ten years, she won commercial success with her photojournalism and fashion and advertising photography, at the same time that she was at the forefront of the artistic scene in Paris.

She combined elements from three different artistic movements in her photography. Art historians have noted that she used the symbolism and dream imagery of the Surrealists; the technological innovations and perspectives of the "New Vision" photography, which included fast film, daring perspectives, use of natural light and geometries, and darkroom techniques of solarisation and cropping; and the documentary photographers' attempts to capture truer records of the world.

She became known for her intricate compositions, which included taking photographs from unusual angles and vantage points. Her artistic eye was aided by her mathematical and scientific background. Sometimes, she told Walter, she turned her photographs upside-down and sideways to assess her compositions. She was fascinated with shadow, light and dark, and geometrical shapes. They talked about the Leica camera, its capabilities, and how much they enjoyed using it. Bing experimented with photographing Paris at night, and used mirrors and reflections to create her compositions. She felt confident in the darkroom and experimented there with enlarging her photographs, cropping, and making multiple exposures.

She did most of her work on a freelance basis for the German and French illustrated magazine industry. When Hitler rose to power in 1933, she told Walter that she refused to work for German magazines. Walter respected her for taking that stance. She took photographs for her own practice, including when she was on assignment with the top publications of that time.

Some of her personal work was in a documentary style like that of Cartier-Bresson. Her photographs were regularly exhibited alongside him, and also with Man Ray and other luminaries. In the 1930's, her work was exhibited at the Louvre, in galleries in Paris, and in New York City at galleries and in the Museum of Modern Art. When visiting New York during that period, she met Alfred Stieglitz, a famous figure in the American photographic world, and she said that her photographs taken after that of City scenes showed his influence. Stieglitz had been promoting photography as an art form for many years, which confirmed Bing's personal views. Walter was impressed with her ambition, but he did not have any for his own work.

Bing married a Jewish pianist and musicologist in 1937. In 1940, she and her husband were expelled from Paris and interned in separate camps in the South of France because they were both Jews. For a six week period she was jailed by the Vichy government at Camp Gurs in the Pyrenees, and eventually rejoined her husband in Marseille. They were finally able to obtain visas with the help of the fashion editor of the magazine, Harpers Bazaar. They left for the United States in June of 1941 and settled in New York City.

Walter asked her what happened to her photographs when she was forced to leave Paris. She said that she took her negatives, but she left her original prints with a friend. After the war, her friend shipped her prints to New York, but Bing was unable to afford the custom fees to retrieve all of them. She had a frenzied time of trying to figure out which ones to keep, and she lost many of the original, vintage prints. Bing recalled that she was saddened by that situation as it was representative of all of the trauma she felt, and all of the losses.

Bing and Walter shared how being expelled, imprisoned, and relocated felt. Walter told her that his having been denied an education, having been imprisoned, tortured and starved, having watched others being tortured and killed, and his experiences fighting in multiple wars, were the most painful parts of his emotional journey from which he could not seem to fully recover from. Although Bing had not suffered in the wartime years as much as Walter had, she too felt she had been ostracized, reviled and damaged. They congratulated each other for surviving all that they had, which they agreed was the ultimate victory, and for remaining married to their original spouses, which in the world of photographers and artists, was unusual.

Bing told Walter that New York City revitalized her art, and was a wonderful place, but she had great difficulty in re-establishing her reputation and getting the important work she had been getting in Paris. She tried to get photojournalism assignments in New York, but found that the competition was fierce because there were many other photographers who had to flee Europe and were seeking work too. She mostly did portraits, and many were of children. She continued to exhibit her photography in the 1940's and 1950's. Although Walter never achieved commercial success, he understood the challenges of having to establish oneself in a new home, of being exiled, of being an outsider, and of being homeless, literally and figuratively.

After she moved to New York, her work conveyed more of a sense of impermanence, alienation, isolation and harshness which reflected her adjustment to her new urban environment. In 1947, she began experimenting using a larger scale with a large-format Rolleiflex camera, and an electronic flash. She later worked exclusively in color, and did her own developing. Walter, on the other hand, stayed with the Leica for his entire career.

By 1959, she stopped photographing as she determined that she had said all she wanted to with the photographic medium and that she had tired of it. She turned, instead, to writing poetry, drawing, and constructing collages which often contained old photographs. She told Walter that it was only in the 1970's that her earlier work in photography was re-discovered, and that she did not receive much recognition for her other artistic work.

Every year after 1976, when Walter came to visit me, he would arrange for a meal with Ilse Bing. She always made herself available to him, as they felt themselves to be kindred spirits. She lived to an old age, remained youthful by riding a bicycle in Manhattan, and groomed dogs to make extra money. She died one year before Walter did, having outlived her husband by about nine years. Walter felt that she should have continued with her photography because of her superior talent, and it saddened him that she felt she had no more to say with it. She never expressed the same regret.

Garry Winogrand

Walter came to New York to visit me the following year, in 1977. I told him that Garry Winogrand, a famous American street photographer, was having a solo exhibition called "Public Relations" at the Museum of Modern Art. Winogrand had been given his second (of three) Guggenheim fellowships to photograph "the effect of media on events." The photographs he took for that project, between 1969 and 1976, were exhibited. It included photographs of marches, demonstrations, strikes, funerals, parades, and many other events of the times. I was able to wrangle an invitation for Walter to attend that opening through my connections. I thought that given his interest in following the news, which he did consistently throughout his life, he would relate to the social issues Winogrand was trying to portray. People in the field were beginning to refer to Winogrand as the "central photographer of his generation."

Despite Walter's lack of formal education, he was an avid reader of newspapers. He read about Winogrand's background and photography in the New York papers. I had a copy of his controversial book, "Women are Beautiful," as well as other published monographs of his photographs. He published seven books during his lifetime, and his photographs had been in many gallery and museum exhibitions. He was known for his chance observations of daily life.

Walter looked at the books of Winogrand's that I had. He appreciated the images of the women, especially, as he remained a hard core "ladies' man." Some reviewers had criticized the images as being vulgar, and took offense that the women seemed to be unaware that their photographs were being taken and were in "questionable positions." Walter was not impacted by or influenced by the women's movement, and he would never have described himself as a feminist. Such an analysis was alien to his way of thinking. Not surprisingly, he did not understand why the feminists had negatively critiqued Winogrand's photographs of women.

Winogrand's work was familiar to Walter for other reasons. Diane Arbus had exhibited with Winogrand, and mentioned him to Walter when she was alive as she and Winogrand were both photographing in New York City in the 1960's. He was best known for his photographs of people, city streets, animals in zoos and rodeos. He compulsively shot photographs of women, his favorite subject. His street photography was a blend of photojournalist and documentary styles. He used a Leica 35mm camera and mounted a wide-angle lens on it.

When Walter attended the opening, he knew who Winogrand was immediately. He was standing in the middle of a crowd of people. He was short, with intense eyes, curly, long, dark hair, a fleshy nose, and thick lips. He had an open, smiley face, with somewhat of a sardonic air about him. He wore a rumpled suit and looked disheveled. Winogrand was about ten years younger than Walter, but he appeared older than his years. In fact, he died at the age of fifty-six of gallbladder cancer, fifteen years before Walter died.

Walter was a master at connecting with people, and getting them to spend time with him. Winogrand was no exception. Walter liked his blunt style, his heavy Bronx accent and his down-to-earth commonness. He also saw a sweetness in him, which Walter had too. They spoke for some time, and agreed to meet at a deli on the lower east side.

At their meeting, Winogrand shared with him that his parents were Jewish, and had emigrated to the United States from Budapest and Warsaw. Winogrand grew up in a predominantly Jewish working-class area of the Bronx. He studied painting and photography in college, and took a photojournalism class. In the 1950's and 1960's, he worked as a photojournalist and advertising photographer, and his work appeared in magazines. His big break came when he was exhibited in the 1955 exhibition called "The Family of Man" at the Museum of Modern Art in New York City.

He told Walter that in the 1970's, he had been supporting himself by teaching, and that he planned to move to Los Angeles. He shared that everyone who knew him described him as "an almost obsessive picture-taking machine." Walter conceded that he never left the house without his camera, and was always taking pictures too.

Walter said that he preferred to take his photographs in black and white, but people had just started preferring colored photographs, and he would have to adjust to it. Winogrand did much of his work in black and white too, but he did produce more than 45,000 color slides between the early 1950's and the late 1960's, although he did not have the money to print them. Thus, he was best known for his black and white photographs.

He told Walter that he took many of his colored photographs in New York City, and also on journeys throughout the United States. He did so with industrially manufactured color film used by commercial and amateur photographers. He asserted that that type of colored film best expressed the aesthetic he was trying to achieve.

Winogrand said that he preferred to take pictures of the American middle class, whether in cities or in suburbs, and that he preferred taking pictures to editing them or producing books and exhibitions. Thus, many of his photographs remained unprocessed. He preferred to take confrontational pictures such that he stood among the participants at events, which matched his turbulent life and the politics of the times. He had the opportunity to do so because of his grants and fellowships. Walter's photographs were mostly of the poor and middle class, and, unless the photographs were paid for in advance, he never processed them as he could not afford to. Walter tried to make his subjects look as attractive as possible so that they were satisfied with his images.

Winogrand described his process of street photography. He said that while he was in a crowd, he would bring the Leica to his eye and drop it away quickly so that people did not know if they were being photographed or not. He did not want to be noticed. He worked without photographic aesthetics, and used virtual automatic photography which was impulsive and improvisational. Walter used the same technique when he was not busy taking posed pictures for work.

Walter asked Winogrand about his controversial book with photographs of women in it. Winograd took pictures of random women in random locations, engaged in a variety of activities. He said, "whenever I've seen an attractive woman, I've done my best to photograph her. I don't know if all the women in the photographs are beautiful, but I do know that the women are beautiful in the photographs." He had confidence in what he could do with a camera, and described himself as a male chauvinist pig.

Walter asked many questions of people he would meet, and he was an intent listener. He was always curious about private lives. Winogrand shared with him that he had been married three times, that he had two children with his first wife, and one child with his third wife. He thought that his third wife was a charm, but that he had issues with leading a conventional life. He said that he knew that he was difficult to live with and admitted that he was irresponsible with money. He owed the government for taxes, he did not pay his rent on time, he had a terrible credit rating, and was always running out of money. He was not meant to live a conventional lifestyle. His heart was in his photographs, twenty thousand rolls of which he had taken and developed over the course of his life.

Winogrand realized that he led a chaotic life. It turns out that he died without seeing a quarter-million of his images, nearly a quarter of his life's work, because four thousand of his rolls of film were not printed, and another twenty-five hundred were never developed. He told Walter that he had trouble completing things, and that he always engaged in furious activity without rest. He believed that most of his work was a failure.

Walter assured him that he was being too pessimistic, and that his work had much value. Walter showed Winogrand some of his prints, and Winogrand was impressed with how he had captured Cologne, Germany, and its people, in a snapshot of time. They parted after the meeting knowing that they would probably never meet again because of geographical distances. Nonetheless, the meeting felt cathartic for both of them. Somehow, despite the chaos of their private lives, they were able to capture fleeting moments and record them in an energetic way, which, at the very least kept them busy, and at the very best consisted of a real contribution. For Walter, he contributed to the people who received his prints since he did not retain them. It was an act of giving.

Cornell Capa

Walter recalled that Ilse Bing told him that while she was in Paris in 1936, she met Cornell Capa through his brother, Robert Capa. Cornell Capa had just escaped from the anti-Semitic climate in Hungary, where the brothers were both born. Robert had arrived in Paris earlier. She had fond memories of their being young people in Paris at the same time, pursuing their dedication to photography. Walter wanted to meet Cornell because he knew his brother, and because Cornell had founded the International Center of Photography in New York in 1974. Bing agreed to make the introduction.

In 1978, Bing and Walter went to meet with Cornell in New York City while Walter was visiting from Germany. They met at the offices of the International Center of Photography. Cornell had white hair, strong features, a cleft chin and dark, bushy eyebrows. He had a kindly but powerful face and bulky build. He exuded energy and warmth.

Walter and Cornell were the same age and were eager to learn more about one another. Bing had heard many of the stories already, but she was a keen listener. There was much pleasure in being in one another's company.

Cornell told them that he was born in Budapest, Austria-Hungary to a Jewish family. His birth name was Cornell Friedmann. They were assimilated and nonpracticing Jews, just as Ilsa and Walter's parents were. Cornell's father owned a prosperous dressmaking salon. Another brother died of a disease so he was familiar with early loss and its effect upon a family.

When Cornell was eighteen years old, after graduating from gymnasium, he moved to Paris to join his elder brother Robert who was working as a photojournalist. He worked as Robert's printer for a year, and made prints, also, for Henri Cartier-Bresson and David Seymour (Chim). Instead of embarking on his medical studies, as he had originally planned, he thought that he could help the most people through photography. He gave up his ambition to become a doctor and he adopted his brother's new last name. He then moved to New York City in 1937 to pursue his photography career. His mother and her four sisters had already moved to New York City. He married in 1940, and he remained married to the same wife until her death. She had helped him to maintain his negatives and archives, as well as Robert Capa's.

Initially, he worked in the darkroom at Life magazine to earn a living. He then served in the United States Airforce, and, after he completed his service, in 1946, he became a Life staff photographer where he remained until 1954. Cornell told us that he arranged with Life to be a photographer for peace, as one war photographer was enough for his family.

He worked on hundreds of assignments for the magazine. The primary focus of his photographic work was social justice and politics. Ilsa remembered his photo essays of Adlai Stevenson's presidential campaign, the education of "mentally retarded" children in New England, the Christian missionaries in the jungles of Latin America and the elite Queen's Guards in England.

He discussed his visit to Caracas, Venezuela in 1953 to create a photo-report, and he fondly recalled his opportunity to photograph the artist and sculptor, Armando Reveron. Ilsa remembered the covers for the magazine that he shot including the portraits of the painter, Grandma Moses, the television personality, Jack Paar, and the actor, Clark Gable.

When they broached the subject of Robert Capa's death, they all became quiet for a bit. Robert had been killed in 1954 by a landmine while covering the final years of the First Indochina War. Cornell discussed how devastating the loss of his brother had been for him. He credited Robert for encouraging him to become a professional photojournalist, and for helping him to obtain his affiliation with Life magazine. He said that Robert's death was a pivotal point in his life, and that he was haunted by what happens to the work after a photographer dies, and how to make the work stay alive.

In 1954, he decided to leave Life magazine to continue the effort his brother had started at Magnum, the international cooperative photography agency Robert had co-founded with Henri Cartier-Bresson, David Seymour (Chim), and George Rodger. Walter shared how much he admired the photographs Robert took in Israel, and how he felt grateful for having had the opportunity to meet him and to spend time with him. Cornell told them that he felt gratified to have written forwards to collections of his brother's photographs, and that he took great pains to protect Robert's reputation and the memory of him.

Cornell determined that working at Magnum was the best activity he could do in honor of his brother's memory and of all he tried to accomplish. When David Seymour (Chim) died in Egypt during a military conflict, while he was reporting on the Suez Crisis for Newsweek magazine, Cornell became the president of Magnum, a position he held until 1960.

While at Magnum, over the next twenty years, Cornell covered many important subjects and events including the Soviet Union and the plight of the Russian Orthodox Church there, the Israeli Six-Day War, American politicians, and old age in America. He photographed the activities and oppression of the Peron government in Argentina and the revolution there, three Democratic National Conventions, and John F. Kennedy's first hundred days in office. He covered the electoral campaigns of John and Robert Kennedy and Nelson Rockefeller.

Cornell said that starting in 1967, he mounted a series of exhibits, and that he published several books. One of his books published in 1968 called "The Concerned Photographer," is emblematic of his philosophy, and defined a photographer as one ". . . who is passionately dedicated to doing work that will contribute to the understanding or the well-being of humanity-work that focuses with compassion, with intelligence, with warmth and generosity of spirit upon the human condition." Cornell acknowledged that his work was eclectic in that he would capture moments in large scale wars, as well as in everyday life. Ironically, one of his most widely known photographs was a 1958 photograph of three ballerinas at the Bolshoi Ballet School in Moscow.

Walter asked Cornell why he became the founder and director of the International Center for Photography in New York City in 1974. Cornell told them that his exhibits led to it. He acknowledged that he had been thinking about how to promote photography and protect photographers' legacies since Robert's death. The goal of the organization was "to bring humanitarian documentary photographic work to the public through exhibition and education, to promote photography as a means of communication and creative expression, and to preserve photographic archives." He spent less time taking his own photographs, and became devoted to promoting other photographers' work. He proudly mentioned that Jacqueline Kennedy Onassis became one of the first trustees. He was gratified that the archives of his brother, Robert Capa, reside at the Center.

Cornell talked about how the word "photography" was coined from Greek words that mean writing with light, and that, through the organization, he wanted to foster respect for photography as an art form. Ilsa could relate to that effort. He asked Ilsa if at some point she would be interested in a retrospective exhibition at the International Center for Photography as she best exemplified photography as an art form. She said she would be willing to be involved in that.

Cornell also said that he was not an artist and that he never intended to be one. Walter related to that statement. Cornell told them that he hoped that he made some good photographs, but he really hoped that he had done some good photo stories with memorable images that made a point, and perhaps, even made a difference.

Walter was not idealistic enough to believe that his own photographs would matter so much. Walter told Cornell about the types of photographs that he took in Cologne, Germany, and his relationship with August Sander. Cornell told Walter to send him some of his photographs. Walter never did. He had no interest in exhibiting or having his work archived, although he did not tell Cornell that and acted as if he was curious about it.

Walter asked Cornell if there were photographers in New York City whom Cornell thought Walter should meet.

Walter was always fascinated to meet all kinds of people, especially artists and outsiders. Cornell told him to look up Garry Winogrand, Helen Levitt, and Alfred Eisenstaedt as he thought that they would inspire him, and vice versa. He gave Walter their contact information, and told Walter that he would contact them and make them aware of Walter's intention. Walter told him that he met Garry Winogrand already, and that Cornell was absolutely correct in that he was an exciting photographer to meet.

Ilse and Walter came away from the meeting feeling inspired by Cornell's charisma, and his dedication to promoting and preserving photography. They felt themselves to be more broken as humans than Cornell was. Cornell transformed the grief he felt about his brother's death, and made it into a cause. His ambition seemed to be boundless, but now it was for other photographers' work and not for his own.

Chapter Eight

Visiting New York in the 1980's

"I had attached to my camera — I had a little device that fit on the Leica camera that they called a winkelsucher, which meant that you could look one way and take the picture the other. You could turn your camera sideways."

–Helen Levitt, American Photographer and Filmmaker

"It is more important to click with people than to click the shutter."

–Alfred Eisenstaedt, German-born American Photographer and Photojournalist

"I went into photography because it seemed like the perfect vehicle for commenting on the madness of today's existence."

–Robert Mapplethorpe, American Photographer

Helen Levitt

In 1981, Walter came to visit me in New York. I had been assigned to interview Helen Levitt, the famous American street photographer of New York City and documentary filmmaker, who was five years older than Walter. Walter begged me to let him come along. He had heard about her from both Walker Evans and Henri Cartier-Bresson, who had been friends with her, and respected her artistry. Cornell Capa had told him to meet her too. I told Walter that he could attend.

We went to her small Greenwich Village apartment, which was a fourth floor walk-up, to conduct the interview. She was in her late sixties, lived alone with her yellow tabby cat, and had never married or had children. The apartment was shabby and tattered. She was extremely shy and introverted, plain and unassuming, but Walter was able to charm her and make her laugh, which made my job easier. She was highly intelligent, with a good sense of humor and enthusiasm about her work. She told us that she did not give many interviews, and that she led a very private and quiet life. I felt honored that she had consented to meet us, and that she did not mind that Walter came too. In fact, I think that his presence put her at ease, as if we were having a mini family gathering.

She proudly told us that she was born and raised in Brooklyn, New York, and that her father was a Russian-Jewish immigrant who ran a wholesale knit-goods business. Her mother had been a bookkeeper prior to her marriage to her father. Like Walter, she was a lifelong supporter of the underdog and disenfranchised.

I asked her when she became interested in photography. She told me that in 1930, when she was a teenager, she saw photographs taken by Henri Cartier-Bresson at the Julien Levy

Gallery, and decided that she would become a photographer too as she became conscious of the fact that photography could be art. Much to the dismay of her parents, she dropped out of high school during her senior year and worked in a portrait studio of a commercial photographer in the Bronx in order to obtain some training. She started out learning how to develop photographs in the darkroom. She also took photographs of her mother's friends for practice with a used camera.

In 1935, when Cartier-Bresson spent a year in New York, Helen met him, and was privileged to spend a day with him photographing along the Brooklyn waterfront. Somehow, even though she was shy, she managed to meet her mentors and to get them to teach her. She learned how to capture everyday life with grace from him. Because of Cartier-Bresson, she was inspired to purchase a second-hand 35-mm Leica camera, and walked around poor and working class neighborhoods in New York City to seek subject matter.

She spent the next forty years taking pictures of the daily activities of women, children, the middle-aged, old people, and minorities in those neighborhoods, including Spanish Harlem, the Garment District, and the Lower East Side. Because there was no air conditioning at that time, people used the streets as their living rooms, and her street photography took advantage of that fact. The street was a stage, and through her photography, she showed how things really were in New York's neighborhoods. She said that she further trained her eye by going to museums and art galleries, because the paintings taught her about composition.

In the mid 1930's, she taught art classes to children. She became fascinated with the chalk drawings that were made by children on the street, and she started to photograph both the drawings and the children with her Leica. In 1938, in a daring move, she went to the studio of Walker Evans and showed him her portfolio. It consisted of photographs of children playing in the street and of chalk graffiti made by them. He was impressed by her photographs, and they became great friends. She studied photography with him for a year. She felt grateful to him for sharing his knowledge with her. She learned how to take spare and direct photographs of commonplace subjects from him, and they went into the subways together and took pictures. Walter told Helen that he did the same thing with him, and how thrilling it was to observe all types of humanity there.

Evans told people that the only photographers who had anything original to say were himself, Cartier-Bresson, and Helen. Helen recalled his saying that with a chuckle. She also met novelist and film critic James Agee through Evans, and made a film with him. She learned to play poker from Agee, and joined a poker group. Walter told her how much he enjoyed playing poker, and they agreed to meet up another time to do so. He told her he could take her to some interesting gambling spots too. I cannot say I was thrilled about that invitation, but that was quintessential Walter to ask her.

She was particularly inspired, also, by a Lithuanian-born American artist, Ben Shahn, who took photographs of life on New York City sidewalks in the 1930's. She said his work helped her to better observe urban life and its possibilities. After having developed her eye, and having learned from other artists, her work was published in magazines, and her career began to flourish.

She focused in large measure on the play life of children on the gritty streets of New York. The photographs were unposed, spontaneous and intimate. Her subjects did not know that they were being photographed as she made herself invisible.

She would turn the Leica sideways to take the picture so that she could meld into the street life. She said that the children inspired her by their ability to create imaginary worlds from simple resources as juxtaposed against their rough surroundings.

I asked her how she felt about being referred to as New York's "visual poet laureate." She blushed profusely. She said she just wanted to capture life as she found it, but recognized that she captured a subjective truth about the world. She was interested in human movement and expressions of the body. She said, impishly, that she "hated kids," but loved to photograph them. She was given her first solo exhibition at the Museum of Modern Art in New York in 1943 entitled "Photographs of Children," which consisted of her photographs of children absorbed in play.

Her photograph of a white little girl and a black little boy playing and dancing in the street has become an iconic image. I asked her what interested her about that subject matter. She said that there was racial segregation at that time, and that there was a great fear of black men in the white community. She wanted to capture two children who were innocent and free from societal prohibitions, and from the upside down world of adults. She said that she was lucky to come upon that moment in 1940 to represent that point of view.

She told us that she continued to be extremely concerned about social and racial inequalities. Walter shared that outlook. They talked about how being an immigrant at some time in your life, and being a Jew, an outsider, heightened one's sensitivity to those issues, although, unfortunately, not all people remembered their heritage. She talked about being a cinematographer for the 1948 film titled "The Quiet One," which she made with James Agee. It dealt with an emotionally troubled black boy in New York City. She worked on other films as well.

She said that she remained concerned with injustice, and that it has been a focus of her professional life. Walter took care of his concerns at the voting booth. Although his photography was not involved in an obvious way with the issue of injustice, some of his images could have been interpreted as dealing with unfairness.

I asked her if she had ever wanted to become a photojournalist, since her photographs required spontaneity and hair-trigger reflexes. She told us that she was too introverted, and that she was not a good technician as she was not interested in that part of photography. She said that she pursued other avenues in order to support herself, including having worked as a film editor. She was an early pioneer of avant garde filmmaking.

Later, in 1959, she returned to still photography to work in color. She received two Guggenheim fellowships to do so. I asked her if we could see her photographs in color. She said that most of that earlier work was lost when her apartment was burglarized, and that she had been trying to make up for it by shooting additional photographs in color since the 1970's. She expressed how traumatized she was by the loss of those negatives and photographs, but the event did not deter her from continuing to shoot. She showed us some of her later colored photographs that, in 1974, were exhibited in her solo show at the Museum of Modern Art. She said that she continued to work in black and white as well, as she had in the 1930's and 1940's.

She told us that she was "re-discovered" in the 1960's due to the feminist movement, and that she had some major shows of her photographs during that period. She was flattered that her work was described as "playful and poetic," while at the same time described as honestly portraying her subjects on the sidewalks and stoops of New York City's tenements. I asked her if she was a feminist, and she replied that she was a person who was against injustice in any and every sphere. Walter probably needed to be educated about feminism, but he did not take an interest in that movement.

I had heard that Helen was born with Meniere's disease, which was an inner-ear disease. I asked her if that ailment had impacted on her work. She said that while she had been dizzy and wobbly her whole life, she did not let that stop her from photographing and dancing, which were her favorite activities. She told us she nearly died of pneumonia in the 1950's, but that did not stop her either. She was intrepid.

She told us that what interfered with her work more than her physical condition was the fact that children used to spend more time outside in the 1940's and 1950's in those close knit neighborhoods than they did presently. The neighborhoods were teeming with activity. People from all walks of life used to come together, with old and middle aged people on the stoops, and young people on the sidewalks and street.

She said that the street was the stage, and the people on it were the actors and actresses, dancers and mimes. That was the art in it for her. She found that street life was less sociable and not as visually interesting at the time we spoke. She bemoaned the fact that the streets were empty, and that people were no longer connecting there. She attributed the change to more television watching, and perhaps air conditioners.

I tried to get her to talk about the art in her photographs more thoroughly. She said, "if it were easy to talk about, I'd be a writer. Since I'm inarticulate, I express myself with images." She told us that she never had a project in mind. She would just go out and shoot, follow her eyes, and what they noticed she would try to capture with her camera for others to see. She said it was an intuitive process rather than an intellectual one, and that the aesthetic was in reality itself. Walter told her he thought that she articulated the process perfectly.

We concluded the interview with a cup of tea, some German jokes which Walter translated for Helen into English, and good feelings all around. In 2009 I heard that she died at the age of ninety-five in her sleep. She deserved a quiet ending to a quiet life filled with great artistic contributions on her part.

Alfred Eisenstaedt

In August of 1988, I took Walter to Martha's Vineyard in Massachusetts for a summer vacation. I had read that Alfred Eisenstaedt, the famous German-born American photographer and photojournalist, spent time there each summer. Eisenstaedt won the International Center for Photography's Infinity Master of Photography Award that year. I had met him at his place of employment, Life Magazine, when I interviewed him in the early 1970's, and it was one of the most memorable interviews I conducted.

He was twenty years older than Walter, but like my father, he was short in stature, and had a warm, kind, and engaging personality. I encouraged Walter to meet him and to see if he could buy some of his photographs. I gave Walter some money for that purpose, and he agreed to look him up. Walter located him in a tiny cottage where he lived, knocked on the door, and their conversation began. Eisenstaedt invited him in with no hesitation.

Their meeting one another was a great opportunity for both of them. I should say at the outset, however, that Walter took the money I gave him and gambled it away, thus, he never returned with any of Eisenstaedt's photographs. Walter did give me a photograph he took of Eisenstaedt from that day, which was wonderful in its own way.

After Eisenstaedt invited Walter into his home, Eisenstaedt began to tell him much about his life. He was raised in Berlin, Germany in a financially comfortable Jewish family after having been born in West Prussia. He was fascinated by photography from a young age. When he was fourteen years old he was given an Eastman Kodak Folding camera with roll film, and he taught himself photography. He had a darkroom in a bathroom in his parents' home. Unlike Walter, he had the opportunity to study at Berlin University, and he then was drafted and served in the German Army in World War I. Both of his legs were injured, he almost lost them, and he became crippled. Walter shared his war stories from later wars, and they both became teary.

After the war, Eisenstaedt's family lost all of their money. He became a button and belt salesman in Berlin to make money, and practiced photography on the side as a freelance photojournalist. He achieved success in his photographic endeavors. In 1928, he took a photograph of Marlene Dietrich in Berlin while she was filming Der Blaue Engel, which was quite a thrill for him. In 1929, he covered the event when Thomas Mann, a German writer, accepted the Nobel Prize in literature.

He told Walter that despite his small stature, he was never intimidated by people who were royalty, famous, rich, or better educated. He treated everyone like a friend, and because of his personality, he put everyone at ease. Walter knew that was an important quality when taking quality portraits. Eisenstaedt was drawn to celebrity. Walter was drawn to the ordinary man.

In 1929, Eisenstaedt sold his first photograph and began his free-lance career for Pacific and Atlantic Photos Agency in Berlin, which later became part of the Associated Press. He took many photographs on assignment of musicians, writers and royalty. At that time he was working with heavy equipment, tripods, and glass plate negatives. He worked, also, for Illustrierte Zeitung, a large publishing house. He began to use the 35-mm Leica camera early on.

Eisenstaedt described to Walter that he photographed the first meeting between Adolf Hitler and Benito Mussolini in Italy, and how terrified he was of Hitler's appeal. He covered Hitler's rise in power. He also took a photograph in 1933 of the Reich Minister of Propaganda of Nazi Germany, Joseph Goebbels, at the League of Nations in Geneva. At first Goebbels was friendly towards him, but when he learned that Eisenstaedt was a Jew, he scowled at him when he took the photograph. He captured that moment with his camera. He went to Ethiopia, before the Italian invasion, and created a series of photographs there.

He and Walter talked about what it does to one's psyche to be reviled and hated the way the Nazis treated the Jews. That same year, in 1935, Eisenstaedt and his family emigrated to the United States due to Nazi oppression, and he became a naturalized citizen. He worked as a freelance photojournalist for American publications. He obtained a job at Life magazine in 1936, where he was on staff with Robert Capa. Unlike Capa, he remained at Life for most of his career, until 1972. He became known for his photojournalism of news events and celebrities.

In the 1930's, he covered Hollywood, and took photographs of stars. He said that the actresses Bette Davis, Katharine Hepburn and Sophia Loren were his favorite subjects. He recalled the joy he took in photographing Marilyn Monroe at her home in 1953, and told Walter that he was mesmerized by her sexuality, femininity and her child-like naivete. Walter was jealous of that opportunity as he had a great appreciation for the female form.

Eisenstaedt was another photographer, like Walter, who continued to use a 35-millimeter Leica camera consistently for its ease of use. He preferred the unposed, candid photograph, in black and white, and had a tendency to use natural light. Walter asked him if his iconic photograph, "VJ Day. The Kiss" from 1945, was his favorite photograph that he had taken. It is an image, shot in Times Square, of a nurse in a white dress being embraced by a sailor as they celebrated the end of World War II. Eisenstaedt said that he did not want to brag, but his photographs were on the cover of ninety-two issues of Life Magazine, and he did 2,500 photo-essays for them, so it was hard to choose.

He asked Walter which was his favorite Eisenstaedt photograph. Walter thought about it for a minute as he did not want to insult him with the wrong choice. He quickly replied that he loved the black and white photograph from 1932 of the waiter at the ice rink at the Grand Hotel in St. Moritz because it was whimsical and joyful. That was his instinctual response. Walter preferred Eisenstaedt's human interest photographs to the hard news images of other photojournalists. Eisenstaedt was pleased that Walter was so familiar with his work.

Walter asked him what his most unusual photo shoot was. He recalled that he was taking photographs of Ernest Hemingway, the writer, in his boat, and he was trying to capture a certain feeling. Hemingway did not want to be directed, became angry, tore his own shirt into shreds, and threatened to throw him overboard. Luckily, he was able to obtain the images he wanted without ending up in the water.

Eisenstaedt was in great shape for his age. Walter asked him how he stayed that way. He said that he lived in Jackson Heights, Queens, New York for most of his time in New York, and despite his leg injuries, he walked daily from his home to the Life offices on Sixth Avenue and 51st Street in Manhattan. As far as his mind was concerned, he said that he continuously conducted photographic experiments to challenge himself. He tried using different lenses, filters and prisms using natural light. He said that his passion for photography kept him engaged and alive, and he remained active in every way.

Walter asked Eisenstaedt if he could take a photograph of him before Walter left his home. Eisenstaedt did not want to do it but he agreed because Walter was so charming and insistent. He understood the type of person who would refuse to take no for an answer. Eisenstaedt was immaculately dressed, had a trim figure, a semitic face, and was mostly bald with a few tufts of white hair. He had the look of an intelligent, cultured, European man. Walter posed him in front of a bookshelf filled with books and mementos from his travels. He joked with him to get him to relax, waited patiently until Eisenstaedt smiled, and took the shot with his Leica camera. He knew it would be a sin to pose him too much, and he took the photograph in natural light. He used black and white film. We were both pleased with the result.

Eisenstaedt continued to photograph until his death in 1995. Like Helen Levitt, he died in his sleep after a life well-lived. He was ninety-six years old. He was another survivor of wartime stresses, and he made the most of his circumstances. Walter wished he had known him earlier when he was struggling in New York.

Robert Mapplethorpe

When Walter came to New York in 1989, he went immediately to St. Vincent's Hospital in Greenwich Village. His long time friend Fred, a gay man, whom he met in Dachau concentration camp, and who lived in Greenwich Village, was diagnosed with AIDS, and was in a hospital room. He had liver failure, a lung infection, and immune system issues. He was about to die. The grief Walter felt was unimaginable, and he cried long and hard with Fred while holding his hand. They had been friends for fifty years. They both had tried to be strong for so long. Now his old friend was fragile, weak, and suffering. There was nothing Walter could do to save him.

Walter recalled Fred's story, and how luck had been with him for decades, but had now run out. Fred and his father planned an escape from Dachau. While Fred was in Dachau, his father convinced Eleanor Roosevelt, then First Lady of the United States, a diplomat, and an activist, to write a letter to allow Fred to emigrate to the United States, which she did. Fred had been involved in a number of international youth groups, and was known to her.

After the letter was procured, Fred's father went to visit him in Dachau. His father signed in, and after the visit, Fred left, signed out as his father, and his father remained in the camp. Fred's father had sacrificed himself for his son. Eventually, Fred's father was released, but by that time, instead of going to the United States, Fred had gone to fight in the Spanish Civil War against the fascists. That was not part of the original plan, but Fred was a youthful activist, and that is what gave life meaning for him.

Somehow Fred survived. He had the letter from Eleanor Roosevelt in hand, which his father had hidden away in a hiding place he told Fred about, and which Fred took with him to Spain. Fred was able to obtain a visa to emigrate to the United States, and he then settled in New York City. He had a full life, and lived proudly as a gay man in his private world in Greenwich Village.

But clearly Fred's time had run out. While at St. Vincent's, Fred became friendly with the well-known photographer, Robert Mapplethorpe, who was dying, also, and was being treated in another room next door. They developed a father-son relationship, and they were able to give one another some comfort. Fred was a survivor, after all, and taught Mapplethorpe all the tricks he used to keep going. The ward was filled with other AIDS patients who were in various stages of decay. It was hell on earth, but the nurses were kind, for the most part, and the patients helped each other when they could.

The day Walter visited, Fred managed to get into a wheelchair, with much assistance, and they went to visit Mapplethorpe. Mapplethorpe was lying in bed. He was extremely pale, had become emaciated, and had aged well beyond his forty-two years. His eyes were large and soulful. Walter made some funny remarks, and was able to get Mapplethorpe to relax and smile. Walter commented about how the staff at the hospital would not give out condoms because it was a Catholic institution. They found it ironic.

Mapplethorpe told them that he was raised in a strict, Catholic, conservative, safe environment in Queens, New York, and that he was one of six children. He escaped from that environment, and never looked back. He said that suburban America was a good place to come from in that it was a good place to leave.

He questioned the church and religion in his art, and often used religious symbolism in his work, but nonetheless he was happy with the cross over his hospital bed as he liked its proportions. He thought of himself as the Devil because of his sinful behavior, and told them that beauty and the Devil are the same thing. Some of the other gay men in the ward kept taking the crosses over their beds down and the nuns and nurses kept putting them back up.

Mapplethorpe told them that he was not going to die, and believed he could beat AIDS. He had not come to terms with it. And yet, he had been working on a biography with an author, and had created a foundation in his name. He wanted the foundation to promote photography and to fund medical research to fight AIDS.

He told them that last year they did a major retrospective of his photography at the Whitney Museum of American Art, and he was able to attend it despite his illness. Mapplethorpe had come a long way since 1969 when he dropped out of art school at Pratt Institute in Brooklyn before attaining his degree. He was not ready, even remotely, for life to be over for him and so many of his friends.

They began to recall earlier times in New York City. Fred had many artists, writers and musician friends who lived in the Chelsea Hotel in the early 1970's, and he and Mapplethorpe reminisced about what it was like when Mapplethorpe lived there with Patti Smith, the artist, poet and musician. Walter said how much he loved the photographs Mapplethorpe took of her for the covers of her albums, and how he opened the world up to an androgynous style.

Mapplethorpe was still close to Smith, and she came to visit him at home and in the hospital since he had become ill. It was a friendship of a lifetime, and he was grateful for it. Fred said that his friendship with Walter was the same and that they understood each other completely even though they did not spend a lot of time together.

They all started talking about photography. Walter described his process with his Leica, and how he mainly took portraits. Mapplethorpe said that he originally used a Polaroid

SX-70 camera, and used those photographs in his collages and then separately. His first solo exhibition was called "Polaroids." He was later given a Hasselblad medium format camera and took photographs of the underground scene in New York. Walter said he once had that camera, but gave it back because he preferred working with a Leica camera.

The subject of street photography came up. Mapplethorpe said that for him it was important to get the consent of the people he photographed. He remarked how the photographs of children that he did were among the most difficult because the photographer could not control them. He said how he loved to do portraits, and he did them of people from every social strata, from royalty, artists and celebrities to "rent boys," who were typically young, gay, male prostitutes. He talked about his time as a staff photographer for Andy Warhol's Interview magazine.

He told them that he relentlessly pursued beauty and perfection in form with whomever and whatever he photographed. He thought about light, shadow, composition and form. He liked to emphasize structure and geometry, and he looked for the perfect symmetry. He sought this when working with his photographic portraits, and with his photographs of nudes, flowers and architecture. Mapplethorpe said that he preferred to work in black and white, primarily in the studio, and that he experimented with different photographic techniques such as photogravures and Cibachrome. Although he liked to photograph a wide range of subjects, his main focus was on erotic imagery.

Mapplethorpe shared that one of his favorite photographs of his own work was of Grace Jones, the Jamaican-American singer, songwriter, model and actress. Andy Warhol had arranged for Mapplethorpe to do the photograph. The artist Keith Haring had decorated her entire face and body with body paint in anticipation of her performance at an alternative dance club in New York City. He felt that it was a wonderful collaboration, and achieved what he had been striving for.

He said that he became especially interested in doing photographic studies of the human figure, harkening back to classical Greek sculpture and the old masters and artists of the Renaissance. He took many photographs of the first World Women's Bodybuilding Champion, and of the male figure, many of whom were athletic black men. He said that he zeroed in on the body part that he considered the most perfect part in that model.

Fred asked him why he did so many self-portraits. He said that he wanted to express, through photography, the part of him that was the most self confident. Many of his photographs had him facing the camera straight on, like an August Sander or Diane Arbus photograph. He had a range of identities which he explored, including one where he looked like a knife-wielding bad boy, and the other where he was a transvestite, wearing make-up and fur. He also took self-portraits after he was diagnosed with AIDS, which showed his deterioration, his suffering, his need for release from it, and his mortality.

Walter told Mapplethorpe that he could not relate to his photographs from the late 1970's in which he documented his friends in the sadomasochism scene. He was shocked by the ones where they were involved in extreme sexual acts, in particular. The Nazi style black leather uniforms they wore were especially jarring for Walter. Fred did not have a problem with any of it. He felt that they were honest explorations of sexuality. He was used to a greater range of sexual behavior having lived in Greenwich Village for so long.

Mapplethorpe countered that he did not like the word shocking to describe his work. He said he was looking for the unexpected, and he felt an obligation to do those pictures. He said that he enjoyed participating in the sexual acts which he was photographing, and that he engaged his models sexually. That was part of his exploration and part of his art. He said that he tried not to be ashamed of his participation in it, but because of his Catholic background, sometimes he was.

He admitted that some of his work was pornographic, and was intended to arouse the viewer, but he hoped, also, that he had achieved art as well. Fred asked Mapplethorpe about his reaction to the debate fueled by the homoeroticism and sado-masochistic themes of some of his work. The controversy was over public funding for the arts, censorship, First Amendment concerns, and the discussions about what is considered art. His detractors were calling his work obscene. Mapplethorpe said that he was not trying to make a political statement in his work, and it had never been his intention to be an icon for either side of the American culture war. He did believe, fervently, however, that his work should never be censored.

Mapplethorpe said how much he wanted to be famous, and how he worked harder and harder on his art once he found out he had AIDS. Despite the controversy surrounding his work, he was pleased that he was exhibited so widely, and talked about so often. Walter and Fred reassured him that he had achieved much more in his lifetime than most people had who lived twice as long. Walter later learned that Fred and Mapplethorpe died on the same day in different hospitals. Walter did not fully understand some of Mapplethorpe's more extreme images, but he believed in his right to express himself, and felt greatly saddened by their deaths.

Chapter Nine

New York in the 1990's

"We have to make room for other people. It's a wheel. You get on. You go to the end. And someone else has the same opportunity to go to the end. And so on. And somebody else takes their place."

–Vivian Maier, American Street Photographer

"Sometimes I think all of my pictures are just pictures of me. My concern is. . .the human predicament; only what I consider the human predicament may simply be my own."

–Richard Avedon, American Fashion and
Portrait Photographer

"My job as a portrait photographer is to seduce, amuse and entertain."

–Helmut Newton, German-Born American
High Fashion Photographer

Vivian Maier

Walter came to New York in 1991. I was busy with work, so he had to fend for himself much of the time. I knew that he went to Atlantic City to gamble quite a bit, but he did not have much money to do it. That activity tapered off when I stopped giving him cash. He began to do his own self-guided tours around Manhattan because when he was not sleeping, he preferred to roam. He was in his early seventies, and had slowed down slightly, but still wanted to explore and entertain himself.

He started taking his lunches in Chinatown because the restaurants were relatively inexpensive, and he could order a variety of steamed and fried buns, dumplings and rolls, along with small dishes and as much black tea as he wanted. He would bring the leftovers home to my mother who spent her day at the apartment. On occasion she would accompany him.

One day he was sitting in one of the restaurants on Mott Street by himself. He observed an eccentric looking woman sitting alone at a table next to him. She appeared as though she might have had money at one time, but no longer did. She was about a decade younger than Walter, he later learned, in her sixties, and she was wearing a floppy hat, a long dress, and men's shoes. Her hair was cut extremely short in a tomboy style. She wore no makeup or jewelry. Despite her wearing a dress, she appeared sexless, prim, and strong. She appeared to be used to dining alone. What drew his attention most was the Leica IIIc camera she wore around her neck.

Walter began a conversation with her. At first she was extremely shy, but Walter was undaunted and could coax anyone to talk. Soon they were sharing a table and engrossed in conversation. He saw, quickly, that she was highly intelligent and opinionated, yet private and reserved. She appeared to have liberal viewpoints about everything. She told Walter that her name was Vivian Maier. She noticed his German accent and asked about his heritage. He gave her his background, which made her more comfortable with him. She shared his socialist leanings, and expressed deep regret for the tortures he had endured because of his religion and politics.

He noticed her French accent, and asked about her background. She told him that her mother was French, her father was Austrian-Hungarian, and she was born in New York City. She spent some of her childhood in France. She said that she learned English mostly by watching movies and going to plays as her mother spoke to her in French. Walter said that his wife had learned English from watching Sesame Street on the television.

She shared that during her childhood she moved to France several times to live with her mother near her mother's relatives. Her father left the family, temporarily, early on, and by the time she was four years old, she lived in the Bronx with her mother and a woman who was a successful portrait photographer. That woman taught her about photography, and instilled in her a life-long passion for it. At one point during her childhood, she lived in New York together with her parents and her brother, but that did not last and she was back in France with her mother again.

Walter told her about how his birth mother had died when he was quite young, and how his father and some of his brothers moved to Brazil because of the Nazis. The dislocation of their families had impacted both of them. They commiserated about how difficult it had been to have little financial, emotional and family stability from a young age.

Vivian described herself as being adventurous, a free spirit, and a loner. She said that she moved from France to New York when she was twenty-five-years-old, and was forced to work in a sweatshop to survive. She found the conditions intolerable. Walter shared how his wife, my mother, had worked in a factory as a slave worker for the Nazis, and later, after the war, in a factory in Germany which made macaroons where she was a virtual slave worker. She too resented that life.

Vivian recalled that five years after working in the sweatshop, she worked as a nanny in New York, and then moved to Chicago and became a nanny for the next forty years for a few affluent families. During her leisure time, she took photographs locally, everywhere she went, and had the opportunity to travel the world on her own taking pictures. She printed the black and white photographs in her makeshift darkroom in one of the homes where she lived as a nanny. The rest of the time, her photographs remained unprinted. She took more than 150,000 photographs during her lifetime, mostly of Chicago, New York City, and Los Angeles.

She said that now she did not have a place to print them, and that all of her negatives and prints were in a storage facility in Chicago. She experimented with color film too, but those rolls were accumulating in storage as well. She said that she never showed anyone her photographs although she had work comprising thousands and thousands of negatives.

She told Walter that she was no longer a nanny for the last family she worked for as the children were grown. She was living in Chicago on her own in humble circumstances and was having difficulty finding other ways to support herself. The children of one of the families she had worked for were helping to pay the rent on her small studio apartment. She was in New York City for a visit, and to take photographs, as it had been some time since her last visit. She had never married or had children of her own, was proudly independent, and did not regret her choices. She said that she had few friends, but that she was not lonely. Her photography filled in the time others spent on social activities.

Walter told her that he had married, and had two sons, but sometimes he wished he had been out on his own, taking photographs, and traveling the world as she had without responsibility for anyone but himself. Most of the time, he said, he liked the closeness of family and friends, and he felt that more than ever he needed his wife to take care of him. He did not feel capable of being as independent as Vivian was.

They started to discuss photography, which they both loved. Walter was wearing his Leica around his neck and told her how he made a living with his photography. Vivian told Walter that when she lived in France in her early twenties, she started taking photographs with a Kodak Brownie camera. A few years later, when she moved back to the United States on her own, she bought a Rolleiflex camera and used it during her leisure time from her jobs. The quality of her photographs dramatically improved with the use of that camera.

Sometimes she would take the children she took care of out of their affluent suburb to take pictures and to expose them to a different life. One time, she took them to the stock yards, where she photographed the bodies of dead sheep with the children looking on. Walter thought that it was strange to expose children to that, but he did not comment or judge. She took many self-portraits, where she would explore her own identity in different environments, and she often photographed her own shadow. She said she enjoyed making homemade films and recordings as well. She preferred clear, calm compositions, without a lot of movement or extreme emotion, which was true to her personality.

She said that she bought a Leica IIIc, and various German SLR cameras, in the 1970's, so that she could shoot in color with Kodak Ektachrome 35mm film. She stopped using her Rolleiflex. Instead of taking pictures of people, she began to take more abstract pictures of found objects, newspapers and graffiti. She started to save items she found in trash bins or lying on the curb. She said that throughout her life she had an obsessive need to take pictures nearly every day.

Vivian and Walter discussed the fact that they gravitated toward the poor and less fortunate in society. They both felt an emotional kinship with people in those circumstances. Vivian said that she took many pictures showing the world of women and children, as she was a feminist. She said that she took many photographs of people on the margins of society, including black maids and "bums" on shop stoops.

She told Walter that she never showed her photographs to others because she did them for herself. She did not take photographs to please other people. She did not take them to achieve notoriety and fame. She did not take them to document people and places in history during particular time periods. It was an activity she loved, and it absorbed her entirely. Walter said that he was a photographer because it gave him independence, he liked to take pictures, and he made some money at it. It was a profession for him. He had no interest in exhibiting his photographs, and in fact, had destroyed his negatives.

Vivian said that she was somewhat of a hoarder of her negatives and found objects, and could not give them up. When she could no longer store them with the families she worked for as a nanny, she kept them in a storage facility. She was having trouble affording the fee for the storage. She did not know why she was saving them. It was a compulsion. She did not know who she was saving them for. The photographs were like her children, as she had none, and represented part of her life's work. She did not want to be the one to get rid of them.

After their dim sum lunch together, Walter gave Vivian his leftovers, a twenty dollar bill to buy herself some meals, and his scarf because she looked like she would be cold walking around New York. He gave her my name and telephone number, and said that if she was ever in trouble, I lived in New York and could help her. She told Walter he was one of the most entertaining and kindest persons she had ever met. He joked with her that if he ever thought of becoming a feminist, it would be because of her.

She never contacted me as she was a proud person. I learned that she died in 2009, ten years after Walter died. She had fallen on the ice, hit her head, and never recovered from it. She was first in a hospital, and then a nursing home before she passed. I never did meet her, but Walter managed to get her to pose for a photograph at the end of their meal together. His photograph brought out the beauty in her.

I learned that she became famous after she died. The boxes of her negatives, prints, audio recordings and 8 mm film were auctioned off, and one of the photo collectors, in particular, helped to make her celebrated by linking his blog to a selection of her photographs on Flickr. Many articles, books and exhibits have been produced of her work. A movie was made about her. I was stunned and saddened. I was stunned because my father and I never knew how talented she was as she was unassuming and did not share her work. I was saddened because she never knew how much her work meant to other people. From what Walter told me, if she were alive, I do not think she would have enjoyed the notoriety. Likely she would have donned a disguise and moved elsewhere so that she could live in peace and obscurity.

Richard Avedon

When Walter came to New York in 1992, I told him that I had an assignment to interview the famous American fashion and portrait photographer, Richard Avedon, who had just become the first staff photographer for The New Yorker magazine after an award winning career. Walter wanted to accompany me because he had heard a lot about Avedon from Diane Arbus when she was alive as she and Avedon had been great friends. Bill Cunningham had spoken to Walter about Avedon's work in admiring terms.

Walter knew that Avedon had broken boundaries in the photographic world, and he was fascinated by that, although he was not particularly interested in fashion per se. He was more interested in Avedon's political photography and his portraits of ordinary people and of certain public figures and celebrities. He also heard from Fred that Avedon was bisexual, which Walter was as well, and that was another attraction for him. It was still a time when many people were hiding their sexuality. I asked permission, and was given the go ahead for Walter to attend.

At the time that we met Avedon, he was sixty-nine years old, and Walter was five years older. They were both still working at their photography. I conducted the interview at his studio which was in a former carriage house on the Upper East Side of Manhattan. Avedon was an impressive looking man. He was trim, he wore stylish glasses, he had a shock of white hair with just the right combination of having been orderly and tousled, and he wore neat, elegant clothing. He exuded energy of a much younger individual, and had an androgynous mix of male and female qualities.

When I introduced Walter, and told Avedon a little bit of his background, Avedon was deferential and respectful towards him. Walter had been concerned that Avedon would act like an elitist because of his famous celebrity clients. It turned out that he was simply a lovely, intellectual, artistic Jewish man. Walter, who knew how to flatter, expressed to Avedon that he admired the fact that Avedon was a force behind photography emerging as a legitimate art form in the 1960's through the 1980's. Walter did not really care about photography being an art form, but he liked Avedon immediately, and wanted Avedon to like him.

I asked Avedon about his background. He told me that he was born in New York City, and had spent his entire life there. His father was a Russian-born Jewish immigrant who through his own hard work ended up creating a successful retail dress business on Fifth Avenue. His mother came from a family that owned a dress-manufacturing business. Fashion was in his genes on both sides, and he was drawn to it too. He and Diane Arbus related to one another not only because of their mutual interest in photography, but because her family owned a department store and were Jews in New York City.

Avedon grew up in financial comfort, but he and his family suffered from tragedy. His younger sister, and early muse, had a psychiatric illness for which she was treated. In her teen years she was diagnosed with schizophrenia. Avedon said that her increasing withdrawal from reality was one of the most difficult experiences of his life. That adversity early on in his life, he believed, gave him sensitivity and emotional awareness which helped him to capture the essence of his subjects for his portraits.

I asked him about his interest in photography. He told me that it began at an early age. When he was twelve-years-old he joined the YMHA camera club. He took an interest in fashion because of the family business, and photographed the clothes in his father's store. When he served in the Merchant Marine during World War II, he made identification portraits of the sailors using his Rolleiflex twin lens camera. He said that after photographing one hundred thousand faces, it occurred to him that he was becoming a photographer.

After completing his military duties, he returned to New York, and attended the New School for Social Research at the Design Laboratory in 1946. He studied there with the art director Alexey Brodovitch for one year, initially creating fashion images. They became close friends, and Brodovitch hired him as a staff photographer for Harper's Bazaar magazine. Avedon quickly became the lead photographer, and he worked there for twenty years. Remarkably, Avedon set up his own commercial studio at the age of twenty-one, which he ran throughout his career, and did free-lance photography for other magazines as well.

I did some research about him, and he confirmed the information. When he first started working for Harper's Bazaar, he did not have a studio there. He was forced to be resourceful and take photographs of models and fashions at all kinds of uncommon locations including on the streets, at nightclubs, on the beach, and at the circus. That creativity and inventiveness contributed to the development of his unique artistic vision which combined commercial photography with art.

He was known for his minimalist aesthetic. He would have his subjects performing an action, or he would crop the frame of the photographs to give them a candid and intimate feel. He required that his models show emotion, which was unusual at that time, and his photographing them in outdoor settings was also revolutionary. Toward the end of the 1950's, he started to do his portraiture work in the studio, where he could use strobe lighting, and be in control of the light.

He eventually covered Fashion Week in France for Harper's Bazaar, and for ten years, he took black and white pictures of models all around the City of Paris where they posed in such locations as streetcars, cabarets, and in cafes. Photographing his models out on location instead of in the studio was pioneering.

I asked him about his staged photo shoot at a circus in 1955. One photograph was called "Dovima with Elephants," in which he had the most famous model of the time wearing a black Dior evening gown posed between two elephants. I reminded him that reviewers have said that it was the most original and iconic fashion photograph of all time. Avedon said that he was a perfectionist, and he was never pleased with how it came out. He thought that the long white silk sash she wore should have been moving in a different direction than in the photograph for the best composition.

I asked him why he left Harper's Bazaar and went to work for Vogue magazine. He said that in 1962 he quit working for Harper's Bazaar because of harsh criticism he faced over his collaboration with models of color for an issue of the magazine. He could not tolerate that, and it was time to leave. He then worked for Vogue for more than twenty years as the lead photographer, and photographed most of the covers from 1973 until late 1988.

We talked about his love of doing formal photographic portraits, which he shot from the very beginning of his career, and continued to. Like Walter, he was fascinated by people's personalities and lives, and he would use photography to reveal their character. Sometimes he would employ props, attitudes, poses, accessories, hairstyles and clothing to help to achieve that goal, in keeping with his aesthetic vision. He told us that his photographs do not go below the surface in that he had great faith in surfaces and that a good one was full of clues. That idea reminded us of August Sander's work.

We talked about how much he enjoyed doing photographs with his large-format 8 x 10 view camera of many notable people including President Dwight D. Eisenhower, Marilyn Monroe, Andy Warhol, Bob Dylan and The Beatles. He talked about how all people are vulnerable and human, no matter how celebrated they are, and he tried to show that quality, and to get to the core of their humanity, when he took their pictures.

I asked him how he was able to capture the spirit of his subjects so well. He said that for some of his portraits, he eliminated props and soft lighting, had his subjects look right into the camera as Diane Arbus did, and used a sheer white background. This minimalist approach helped him to get to the essence of his subjects.

He would talk with the subjects while he was taking their pictures to put them at ease. Then he would ask uncomfortable questions and probe them psychologically to evoke reactions. He and Walter talked about how important it was to have rapport with the subjects to achieve the best photographs. Both of them were conversationalists, and knew how to open people's minds and hearts by making them feel safe, while at the same time challenged.

During the 1960's, he took photographs which were more political in nature, including portraits of Dr. Martin Luther King, Jr., Malcolm X, Julian Bond, and the Chicago Seven. He also took pictures of segregationists such as Alabama Governor George Wallace, and everyday people involved in demonstrations.

He said that his advertising photography, however, provided him with a living. He did "brand-defining" photographic work for different companies out of his own studio, including

Calvin Klein, Revlon, Versace, and dozens more. For instance, he was responsible for photographing fifteen-year-old Brooke Shields in sexy poses for the Calvin Klein jeans campaign. The ads were controversial. Some people felt that the images contributed to the decline in morality and destruction of innocence in our society. Avedon did not look at it that way. He thought that they were eye-catching and aesthetically pleasing. He was comfortable with sexuality, and he did not believe that Brooke Shields was compromised in any way by participating in the photograph.

Because he did so well with his commercial photography, including his images for many successful advertising campaigns, he was free to pursue other extended portraiture projects beyond fashion and celebrity. His range was wide. In 1963-1964, he took photographs of the civil rights movement in the American South.

During the Vietnam War, in 1969, he took a series of portraits including those of politicians, American soldiers, victims of the war in the United States and in Vietnam, including Vietnamese napalm victims, protestors, students, counter-cultural artists, cultural dissidents, and activists. He also took photographs of the fall of the Berlin Wall, and of patients in mental hospitals. He said that his work in the mental hospitals was extremely emotionally taxing because of his strong feelings about his mentally ill sister.

I asked Avedon about his series of photographs of his father, which chronicled his father's losing battle with cancer. He said that he had a complicated relationship with his father, and taking the photographs was one way to work out his grief and to connect with his father at the end of his life. He felt that his father, likewise, enjoyed the attention he bestowed on him. The best way he knew how to show his love was by taking photographs. He knew that people criticized the images as being exploitative, but neither he nor his father felt that way, and to him, that was what was important.

Another series which Avedon was known for was called "In the American West." The photographs were taken between 1979 and 1985 pursuant to a commission he received from the Carter Museum of American Art. He did large prints, which sometimes measured over three feet in height. Avedon told us that he did portrait work of ordinary people who represented working-class America, including housewives, farmers and miners, drifters and cowboys. He wanted to show their dignity. The photographs were part of an exhibit, and were made into a book which became a bestseller.

Avedon told us that because of his own health issues in 1974, consisting of serious heart inflammations, his work on his take of the American West became a critical point in his career. His interest in the subject matter had something to do with his feelings of mortality. He was an intellectual at heart, and he wanted to do what he considered to be more substantive work.

These were not traditional portraits of celebrities or beautiful Western scenery, and he was proud of the opportunity to do them. He travelled with his crew, and photographed 762 people with them. They went to many different locations to find their subjects including prisons, rodeos, carnivals, oil fields, coal mines, slaughter houses and other venues. Because he had a sense of his limited time left, he wanted to do something important, and discovering the inner lives of his rural subjects met that goal.

Again, he was criticized for exploiting his subjects and for falsifying the West. Some critics questioned why a photographer from the East Coast who had famous clients would try to capture the suffering of working class people. The detractors accused him of trying to evoke condescending emotions. Avedon told us that there will always be denigrators of artistic work. His intentions were genuine. He felt that he, and others, were capable of a greater range in their art, and should not be limited by such narrow viewpoints. He maintained that it was some of his best work, and he reminded us of the photographs he did in the 1960's of different strata of society. He never intended to be pigeon-holed, as he worked across genres.

He talked about his time as a photographer for Vogue magazine between 1966 and 1990. He told us that some of the photographs he took were controversial and provocative with nudity and themes of violence and death in them. He resisted being censored. He said, ironically, that there is no such thing as inaccuracy in a photograph, that all photographs are accurate, and none of them is the truth.

He expressed gratitude for the opportunity to do portraits of important cultural and political people, including Stephen Sondheim, an American composer and lyricist; Toni Morrison, an American novelist; and Hillary Clinton, a politician.

We arrived at the portion of the interview where we discussed his new position, as of 1992, as the first staff photographer for The New Yorker. He said that he had photographed just about everyone in the world, but he hoped to photograph people of accomplishment, not celebrity, in order to help define the difference once again. We wished him well with his new endeavor.

He told us that many of his photographic books were published throughout his life, and he hoped we would look at them. He said how much he enjoyed working with Truman Capote on his first book of photographs published in 1959. Capote provided text. He also highlighted his book of photography published in 1964 which contained an essay by James Baldwin, a famous black novelist, who became his friend in high school, and remained a life-long friend. I told him that I had both of the books at home. He was pleased.

Toward the end of the interview, I asked him how he felt about Fred Astaire playing a character based on Avedon's life in the 1957 film called "Funny Face." He said that he was just a Jewish boy who liked to make art with his camera. Other people's view of him as a cultural force was their idea.

Walter started to ask Avedon about his personal life just before we left. I was not going to broach the subject or include it in the interview, but Avedon seemed to want to open up to Walter. He said that when he was twenty-one years old he was married, had no children, and divorced five years later. Avedon's bi-sexuality at that time became an issue and she left him. Two years later he married again, and they had one son. They were still married at the time of the interview, but he said the marriage was not blissful. He did not want me to print that. He said that there were rumors about his affairs with men, but he did not want to discuss them for the sake of his wife and child. He wanted his private life to remain private, and I agreed that I would not put any information about his private life or sexuality in my article.

Walter shared with Avedon that he too was bi-sexual, but had been married to my mother for many years, and their relationship remained stable and happy. He felt he was too old for affairs now, and had settled down a bit in that department. I was not pleased to be present while he was sharing that information. Walter said that people had to be free to be themselves, especially toward the end of life, but he could understand why Avedon did not want to share that part of himself with the world, which was still homophobic. Walter talked about his time in a concentration camp, the case against him and his felony conviction for being a homosexual, and about all of the discrimination against Jews and homosexuals in Germany at that time.

As we were about to leave, Avedon gave Walter a print of Marilyn Monroe he had made. He said that she epitomized sexuality, vulnerability and sensitivity. He thought of Walter having those characteristics too. He told Walter that he knew that Walter valued his photographs of ordinary people more, but he thought he might have some fun having Marilyn's photograph on his wall, especially since she was a gay icon.

Avedon died five years after Walter did. Avedon was eighty-years-old at the time, and was on location shooting an assignment for The New Yorker. I learned that he set up The Richard Avedon Foundation during his lifetime, which serves as a repository for all of his work, and organizes publications, exhibitions, and outreach to the academic community. I have covered many of his exhibits, and I can never get enough of his artistry. Walter valued the chance to have met Avedon, a man of exceptional caliber. I did not regret taking Walter with me for that interview.

Helmut Newton

The year before Walter died, in 1998, he came to New York one last time before he died in 1999. At that point he was coughing and weakened, but he still had the strength and inclination to walk around New York City. One weekend, we found ourselves on the Upper East Side. We stepped into a diner on 79th Street and Madison Avenue for a late breakfast. I immediately spotted Helmut Newton and his wife, also a photographer and

former actress and model, whose professional name was Alice
Springs. I met them a few years before when I interviewed him
in Germany regarding one of his photography exhibits.

We went over to them, and they invited us to sit with
them in their booth. They were in New York for a long
weekend holiday. They were returning to Monaco where they
had one of their homes, from California where they had another home. Newton, who was only a few years younger than
Walter, and his wife of some fifty years, who was close in age to
him, were neat and smart in appearance. They were curious to
meet Walter because of his German background and because
he was a photographer.

Newton told Walter that he was born in Berlin as Helmut
Neustadter, his family was Jewish, and his father had been a
button and buckle factory owner. He attended gymnasium
and learned English when he attended the American School
in Berlin. When he was twelve-years-old, he was given his first
camera, and he became obsessed with taking pictures, often
neglecting his school work.

When he was a teenager, he had an apprenticeship with
a woman theatre photographer in Berlin and began to hone
his craft. He sadly told us that the life of his family was ripped
apart when his father's factory was seized by the Nazis, and his
father was taken, briefly, to a concentration camp. In 1938, his
parents fled to Argentina. Newton obtained a passport after
turning eighteen, and left Germany by boat with other Jews
who were escaping from the Nazis. He ended up in Singapore,
where he worked as a photographer.

He was then interned by British authorities, and was sent
to Australia in 1940. He worked as a fruit picker, and later as
a truck driver when he was enlisted in the Australian Army.
After the war, he became a British subject and changed his

name to Newton. Walter told him that some of his family had escaped to Australia, but they ended up in Palestine, which later became Israel. Walter spoke to Newton briefly in German describing what he and his family went through during World War II. They acknowledged to one another how lucky their families were to have escaped when they did.

His wife told us that she met Newton in Australia when she was an actress and model, and that she modeled for him. They fell in love, married in 1948, and have been together ever since. She told us a story about when Newton became ill one day, and asked her to cover his assignment for him because he could not postpone it. He taught her a little bit about photography, and she took over the shoot. All went well.

After that, she learned everything she could about photography, and her passion for it grew exponentially. When she decided to become a photographer too, Newton wanted her to use another last name professionally so that there would not be any confusion in case she did not become a successful photographer. She said that it turned out that he should not have been worried. She winked at us after she said that. She maintained that one famous Newton was enough for one family, and she did not mind that he was the one in the spotlight. She had obtained a lot of good commercial work, and she was satisfied with their life together, her professional life, and her role as his promoter.

Newton told us that at first he had a studio in Melbourne, Australia where he worked on fashion, theatre and industrial photography. Later, in the late 1950's, he landed a contract with British Vogue and left for London, and then eventually ended up in Paris, where he and his wife settled. He continued to work as a fashion photographer for such magazines as French Vogue, Harper's Bazaar, Elle and Playboy, and traveled frequently to locations throughout the world on assignment. He preferred to work in black and white. He photographed such famous models as Cindy Crawford and Charlotte Rampling. Newton was famous, also, for working with long-legged, high-heeled models who were scantily clad.

Walter asked his wife how she felt about his style of using dramatic lighting and posing models nude or suggestively clothed in racy, edgy, erotically charged scenes which had the look of sado-masochism and fetishism. She said that to her it was art, similar to film noir and surrealism, although it was not the style of photography she chose to do.

She said that Newton was comfortable with the themes of sexuality and desire in his work, and he had revolutionized high-fashion photography by dealing with it. She did not agree with the feminists' critiques that Newton's work was overly suggestive, and unnecessarily so. She did not mind that he was called "the King of Kink," as he was daring and exploratory in his images of the human condition. Walter agreed that sometimes Americans are prudish in a way that Europeans are not, especially when there is nudity.

She told us that she has been, and will always be Newton's biggest supporter and promoter. She reminded them that in 1995, she made a film about Helmut which was entitled "Helmut by June." June Browne was her real name. She proudly told us that Helmut had taken the photographic portraits of all the major individuals of his time, from film stars to politicians. She said that to have a portrait done by Newton was the sign of success in whatever field you were in.

Even though Newton had some health challenges, during the 1970's she pushed him to create his own personal art dealing with those themes. Ultimately it resulted in the publication of multiple photography books of his pictures.

Newton acknowledged the important part his wife had played in his success. He told us, in no uncertain terms, that he wanted to be provocative and to take a subversive approach to his photographs. He grew up in "free-thinking" Berlin with surrealism as a theme, which he employed in his commercial photographs. He said that the women models he photographed had to have a certain look of availability, as he believed that women who gave the appearance of being available were sexually more exciting than a woman who was completely distant. He was looking to find the erotic, and he was visualizing his personal obsessions. His wife approved of all he did.

He told us that, especially beginning in the 1970's, after the sexual liberation of the 1960's and the loosening of sexual morality, he explored male and female power relationships and female emancipation in that time of social change. He was looking for a new and different contemporary female image. He was exploring the idea that women's sexuality gave them power. He intended that his photographs should be voyeuristic in nature.

His photographs were mostly shot on location, in elegant villas, mansions, or distinguished hotels. He staged women who looked like they had taken control of the situation, whether they were naked or clothed. Critics said it was ironic that he was showing the decadence of a social class that was largely characterized by power and money.

He explored high and low brow art forms. He tapped into S & M, surrealism, Expressionist cinema, and his love of Film Noir cinema. For him that meant using black and white photography, seductive women, highly posed scenes, and glamorous attire in order to convey emotion. He liked to tell stories with his fashion photography, and to blend the worlds of erotic and fashion photography.

By taking a lot of his photography out on location instead of in the studio, he was expressing the vitality of the street which made his work immediate and dynamic. He told us that a woman does not live in front of a white paper. She lives on the street, in a motor car, and in a hotel room. He was looking to show human interest by bringing a journalistic element to his work, which, for his time, was revolutionary.

Walter loved to look at photographs of women, and promised Newton that he would look at his books, and would look at his wife's work as well. He promised to send some of his shots from Cologne, particularly of prostitutes. After our brunch with them was finished, Helmut told Walter that he would contact him the next time they were in Berlin, and Walter could come to visit them from Cologne. That never happened as Walter became quite ill soon after. Walter and I agreed that the time with Newton, with the added bonus of having met his wife, was satisfying on every level.

Epilogue

At our last meeting at his bedside, Walter asked me to take out the few hundred photographs he had saved of his pictures, which were in a box in his closet in my parents' bedroom. He had thrown out a quarter million negatives and thousands of prints he had taken over the course of his lifetime. Together, we went through the prints that remained.

He picked out twelve of them that he liked the best or which had special meaning for him. I told him that I would keep the photographs in a safe place, and that it would comfort me to have them near and to look at them.

After my father recalled all of the stories I have chronicled, and more, sometimes with my filling in the details of events we shared together, he gave the impression that his body was ready to die, but his mind was not ready. He wanted to admit certain things, perhaps so I would not find them out from someone else after he died. We both felt closer going through all of his recollections, but we did not express that to one another. I did not care if the stories were true or not. I knew he did not either. He just wanted me to know a little more about his real life, and his imagined one. He loved to tell tales, tall and otherwise. The combination helped me to know him better than I ever had.

I was grateful for that. I will never try to sort out reality from fantasy, even if it were possible.

I asked Walter if it would be acceptable to him if I recited a Jewish deathbed confessional prayer called the Viddui, which acknowledges the imperfections of the dying person and seeks a final reconciliation with God. Ironically, neither Walter nor myself were religious Jews, but I thought that it might be a comfort to us to do it as it was an affirmation of our Jewish identity. We recited a few words of prayer together, which I had written, and then cried together.

At the end of my time by his bedside, he started to grow quiet. He seemed exhausted and wanted to sleep all the time. He stopped wanting to take care of himself, and the caregiver had great difficulty getting him to eat, shower, or use the bedpan. He started to retreat inside of himself. My mother and brother could no longer reach him.

He was not interested in saying loving words to anyone, nor did he make any requests to see his many friends. I had to return to New York for an assignment as I had spent many weeks by his side and his doctors could not predict how much longer he had to live. After I returned to New York, I received a call that shortly after I left he had passed away peacefully in his sleep at home, as he had requested. They gave him drugs to ease the pain, and everyone said that at that point he was ready to go physically and mentally. Perhaps he wanted to spare me having to say a final goodbye.

I was relieved that we spent that concentrated time together, as I did not want to feel the guilt of a son who lived far away from his parents. I did not want too many unanswered questions. I do not believe that much was left unsaid. I was able to express to him how deeply I loved him, and I appreciated that many do not get that opportunity before their loved ones die.

I was enormously saddened that I would no longer have him around as he had such a zest for life, a curiosity about people, and a desire to live life to the fullest when he could. I felt the loss every day. I forgave him many times over for how he might have fallen short as a father or as a human being. I know he meant well, and only wanted the best for me and others. He had some vices, but he was never mean or cruel intentionally. He never withheld love. He was simply trying to survive as best he could.

Now I have my memories of him and some of his photographs which he did not destroy. After he died and I decided to write this book, I knew that I would have to include the ten photographs he chose, which are the ones you see here. My mother approved of what I wrote about Walter and of the photographs chosen. Like Helmut Newton's wife, she remained a steadfast supporter of Walter and all that he did from the day she met him until the day she died.

Walter did not think much of his own work, as I emphasized throughout this book, but he has been a continued inspiration to me. Every time I take a photograph, I think of what he taught me about photography and life. My hope is that others will join me in my appreciation for his photographic efforts, which spanned seven decades, for his bravery in facing some of the darkest moments of history, and for his ability to still find joy in life and with his family after having survived it all.

Afterword

The character of Walter is based upon a real person, gleaned from what I heard about him from his relatives and friends. I changed some details, but many of the stories are true, if that is a descriptor, as there are always so many different perspectives. Some of the stories about his meetings with famous photographers are imaginary, except that he did meet Robert Capa in Israel, he knew and was friendly with August Sander for many years in Cologne, and he met Alfred Eisenstaedt in New York City, although what happened during those meetings was sheer fantasy.

The challenge for me, as the author, was to imagine which famous photographers of his time Walter would most like to have met; what he would have wanted to discuss with them; how they would have gotten along; and what they would have said to one another about life and art. It was rewarding to stand in Walter's shoes, because he always got on well with people, was curious about them, was a good listener, and often brought an element of spontaneity to whatever he did. Walter treated everyone the same, whether they were famous and wealthy or unknown and homeless. He was completely comfortable speaking with all individuals. That was true of the real and imaginary Walter.

With the issues regarding immigration dominating today's headlines, the stories of Walter and of many of these photographers are particularly relevant. A large proportion of them were Jewish, or were impacted by the Nazis, had to flee their country to escape persecution, and had to learn different languages, adapt to new cultures, start a life, and find a way to support themselves. Challenges continued into the next generation.

For those with an artistic bent, photography was the perfect way to combine innate artistry with a way to make a living. Not much equipment was required, especially with the Leica camera; the streets, in many cases, could serve as the studio; no formal education was necessary; you could learn on the job; and if you hustled, you could make a living. Women and gay photographers had additional hurdles, and when combined with the immigrant experience, their bravery was admirable and their challenges many.

As I learned about Walter and the other photographers, there were certain recurring themes which I noticed. Most of them started taking photographs when they were young, and had a life-long passion for it, or, in a few instances, it morphed into pursuing another art form in the latter years of their life. They never stopped being creative. Taking pictures was equivalent to breathing for them.

Many of them were liberal in their way of looking at the world and in their politics. There was more acceptance on their part of gender fluidity, sexuality, sexual experimentation, nudity, and what would be considered by some as deviant morality. Most did not stay married to the same person for their lifetime, although Walter was an exception. They were open to experiences in their lives and in their work that often defied society's expectations of proper behavior.

It seemed that they shared certain personality traits as well. They had to be superior salespersons of themselves and their work if they were operating on a professional level, even if they were introverted. Many valued their independence, were adventurous, rebellious, individualistic, liberal, and did not follow rules blindly. They, for the most part, preferred to express themselves visually. They had a sensitivity which enabled them to see beauty and the extraordinary in what for the rest of us might seem as ordinary at first glance. Some were able to show us the seedier sides of life with brutal honesty. They were able to paint with light with their cameras, as they had superior abilities with composition, form, light and shadow, and other elements of their art.

Many of them wanted to make a statement with their photographs, particularly about people whom were less fortunate or events which impacted upon the human experience. This showed a generosity of spirit, and, in some cases, a desire to be famous to get out of their ghetto, real or imagined.

Commercial photographers often pursued celebrities and public figures to achieve their own immortality along with the subject. Most of them wanted to share their visions with people beyond whom they photographed, in the form of exhibits and books of their work. Walter, however, was content if his customers were pleased with their portraits, and did not want to venture into any other realms.

Whether the photographers were taking their pictures for others, or for themselves, they all had a need to express themselves through their own lens and their own vision. Walter was no exception. The photographs in this book were actually taken by the real "Walter."

I want to thank Amos Grunebaum and Rae Ellen Vitiello for their early readings of this book and for their astute comments and edits. I am grateful for insights and recollections from Beny Mendelovits. I want to thank Walter, also, for having been a singular and compelling character and for providing me with many hours of stimulation. Finally, I want to thank Walter's wife and children for standing by him, and for putting up with all of his foibles and flaws, probably because, despite it all, he was able to give and to receive love, a capacity which no concentration camp or any other adverse experience or setback could take away from him.

About the Author

Susan L. Pollet lives in New York City, and has been an attorney for over forty years, primarily in the area of family law. She has published over sixty articles on varied legal topics, including family and criminal law. She was President of the Westchester Women's Bar Association, Vice President of the Women's Bar Association of the State of New York, Executive Director of Pace Women's Justice Center, Director of the New York State Parent Education and Awareness Program, and a prosecutor. She has a strong desire to provide the public with information about interesting people who give us hope.

She is also a published author and artist. In 2019, her first novel was published by Adelaide Books entitled *Lessons in Survival: All About Amos.* She created the collage for the book cover, and also painted the portrait which appears on the cover of this novel. Two of her short stories were published by Adelaide Books in 2019 and 2020 in their literary award anthologies. In 2020, her novel, *Women in Crisis: Stories from the Edge* will be published by Adclaide.

www.ingramcontent.com/pod-product-compliance
Lightning Source LLC
Chambersburg PA
CBHW020020030726
47499CB00007B/2190